★

"He might be sleeping off a few beers too many. Can't hurt to knock. And, Dorothy, if he isn't home, all is not lost. We could finally get into Kevin's house."

He put the cat down gently and banged on the door. There was no response, but the door swung open. "He hasn't repaired that catch yet."

"Would it be okay to go in and find some cat food, do you think?" I reached down to pet the black cat, who had approached with great dignity and an imperious look. "Jerry wouldn't mind."

"No. Wait." Alan's voice was sharp, curt, official. "Don't come closer, Dorothy."

"What—?" I stopped and swallowed hard. The smell had reached me.

Jerry's trailer hadn't smelled good the first time, but the stench now was infinitely worse. Sickly sweet, catching at the throat... I swallowed again. The smell of rotten meat. Or...

 ★

"Dams writes with a good ear for Midwestern dialogue and develops her characters lovingly."
—*Publishers Weekly*

"New readers will feel compelled to read all the Dorothy Martin mysteries, while followers will be anxious for her next exploit."
—*ForeWord*

KILLING CASSIDY

JEANNE M. DAMS

W🌐RLDWIDE.

TORONTO • NEW YORK • LONDON
AMSTERDAM • PARIS • SYDNEY • HAMBURG
STOCKHOLM • ATHENS • TOKYO • MILAN
MADRID • WARSAW • BUDAPEST • AUCKLAND

KILLING CASSIDY

A Worldwide Mystery/November 2001

Published by arrangement with Walker Publishing Company, Inc.

ISBN 0-373-26402-X

Printed in U.S.A.

This book is dedicated to Luci Zahray, whose encyclopedic knowledge of toxicology has helped me with many plots, and who worked this one out virtually single-handedly. She is an avid Sherlockian and a mystery fan without parallel, and I consider myself fortunate to call her my friend.

Author's Note

Most of this book is set near Madison, Indiana, a beautiful little town on the Ohio River. My husband and I love Madison and have visited there frequently. I've rearranged its geography slightly, but I've tried to preserve its unique flavor.

I've erected the town of Hillsburg and Randolph University a few miles northwest of Madison. Neither town nor university bears any resemblance to Hanover or Hanover College, which are real places just west of Madison.

The Tour of Homes is a real Madison event, held every other October and every Christmas. I've altered some details for the October tour to suit my purposes, and moved at least one house so as to fit nicely into the tour, but every house I mention really exists. So far as I am aware, no murderers have ever tried to elude their pursuers during the tour—but of course one never knows.

Beanblossom, Indiana, is a real place, but in a different part of the state. It has no church even remotely like the Full Gospel Church of the Redeeming Spirit, nor have I ever encountered, anywhere, any church like the Church of the All-Consuming Fire—thank goodness.

ONE

"ALAN, LOOK AT this!"

I waved the letter I held in my hand. One of the nice little benefits of living in England is the mail. It arrives early enough in the morning to be consumed with breakfast, and with a predictable regularity that is unknown in America. Or at least it's nice when there's something more interesting than bills, as there certainly was this morning.

Alan lowered the *Times* and took the letter, while I poured myself a second cup of tea and spread marmalade on my toast. We were breakfasting in our kitchen, the coziest room in the Jacobean cottage we both love so much. The sun shone through leaded glass windows and sparkled on the geraniums on the windowsill. Esmeralda and Samantha, our two cats, were outside napping in the sun and trying to ignore the raucous cries of the magpies. The cats hate the magpies, and I have to admit myself that they're messy, noisy, thieving rascals, but I can't help liking them; they're so handsome in their black-and-white livery, and so very English.

Alan read my letter aloud. "'Dear Mrs. Nesbitt.'" He paused for a moment to smile at me. "Has a nice ring to it, doesn't it?"

I grinned back idiotically. We'd been married nearly two years now, but we still weren't quite used to it. One might think that a pair of widowed sixty-somethings would react to marriage with more decorum than is usually exhibited by sweet young things. One might be wrong. I don't actually use my husband's name, feeling more comfortable with the name I used for over forty years, but people often make the natural mistake, and Alan was right. It sounded good.

He went on. "'It is my sad duty to report to you the death of Dr. Kevin Cassidy, who was, I understand, a very old friend of you and your late husband.'"

"In both senses," I replied to his quirked eyebrow. "Frank and I had known him forever, and he was in his nineties. The chairman of biology at Randolph when Frank first went to teach there, and one of our dearest friends. He retired ages ago, of course. He was very kind when Frank died, but when I moved over here I—oh, I don't know, I didn't write very often, and neither did he, and after a while we lost touch, except for Christmas cards. I suppose it's been over a year...." I sighed. Why do we forget about our friends' mortality? Why do we assume we can always make up for lost time? Another sigh. "Go on, get to the next part."

"'...pneumonia...not unexpected...merciful release... rather an unusual clause in his will.' Ah, we're getting to it. 'Bequeathed to you the sum of five thousand dollars, tax free, with the stipulation that you must return to Hillsburg to collect it. Should you fail to comply with this stipulation, the money is to go to the Full Gospel Church of the Redeeming Spirit in Beanblossom.' What in the name of all that's holy is that?"

I made a face. "I'm not sure holiness has anything to do with it. They do various odd things with snakes, I'm told, if indeed the church is still in existence. Beanblossom is a tiny town not far from Hillsburg. More of a wide spot in the road, actually. Nothing thrives in Bean-blossom, or not for long. But the point is that dear old Kevin and I used to have a sort of standing joke about the place and its remarkable theology. It was rather rude of us, I suppose, but he knew quite well that one way to make sure I accepted his bequest was to threaten to give the money to them. I wonder what they'd do with it? Buy bigger and better snakes?''

Alan grinned and went back to the letter. '''—not a large sum of money, of course, but Dr. Cassidy also stipulated that your travel expenses were to be paid by his estate, should you choose to accept his conditions.' This fellow ought to be writing television scripts.''

"Woman. Look at the signature.''

"Ah, yes. Michelle Carmichael. To continue: 'In order to comply with these conditions, you must make arrangements to arrive in Hillsburg within one month of his death, which took place yesterday.' But the letter's dated ninth December—''

"No, it isn't. American-style dating. The month comes first. Nine twelve means September twelfth. Four days ago. So the poor old dear died last Monday. Alan, I'm so sorry I'll never see him again. I owe him a lot.''

I took a sip of my cold tea and leaned my elbows on the table, remembering. "We never had children, Frank and I. You know that. But I did have a—I was never sure what to call it. A false pregnancy or a miscarriage or something. For nearly three months I had all the symptoms of pregnancy, and we were wildly happy. I was over forty and we had just about given up hope. I'd been to the doctor and had the test, and it had come back negative, but the tests are sometimes wrong, and I was so sure. And then—well, then the dream fell apart.

I had what almost amounted to a hemorrhage, and my body went back to normal again.''

I sipped some more tea. Alan moved his hand to cover mine. "My body went back to normal, but not my mind. I couldn't stop crying. I would go to school in the morning, dreading a day of teaching, and I would see all those lovely, healthy children, and I couldn't stand it. After a month or so I was in such a state I had to take a leave of absence, but then I was alone all day with nothing to do but mourn. I couldn't talk to Frank about it. He was unhappy, too, but he buried himself in his work, the way a man will.

"I really think I would have collapsed completely if it hadn't been for Kevin. He saw Frank every day, of course, and he knew something was wrong. So he came and made me tell him what it was. And then he listened. Dear man, I cried all over him, and he hated to see women cry, but he just handed me Kleenex until I was finally all cried out. Then he made me take something for the raging headache I had after all that crying, and *then* he gave me a good old-fashioned talking-to. Told me it wasn't the end of the world, that I had a job I loved and a husband who adored me and a beautiful world to live in, and I should count my blessings. I was in no mood to listen to good advice, but he did something more practical. He went and got the liveliest, naughtiest kitten he could find and gave it to me."

Alan chuckled.

"A kitten refuses to be ignored. If I was tempted to spend the morning in bed feeling sorry for myself, the little demon would come and pounce on my toes with those razor-sharp claws. Or she'd climb the curtains or knock things off the dresser or—oh, you know all the kinds of trouble kittens can find to get into. So I'd *have* to get out of bed, and I'd have to get dressed, too. Jezebel's claws would go right through a bathrobe.''

"Jezebel?''

"Because she was so wicked and so beguiling. Once she had my undivided attention, she'd climb into my lap and lick my hand and be such a sweet kitty. Then she'd purr herself to sleep and nap until she was refreshed and ready to torment me again. She wore me out, chasing after her and cleaning up when she created some disaster—which was frequently—and I began to sleep again nights. And when Frank came home, we'd have Jezebel's antics to laugh about, instead of spending the evening in painful silence avoiding the topic we couldn't discuss. After a couple of weeks I was more than ready to get back to the classroom and thirty-seven children who could not, between them, create anything like as much chaos as three pounds of frisky feline.

"So you see, Kevin saved my sanity. He was an invaluable friend. And unless he failed badly in the last year or so, that part about 'a merciful release' is hogwash. His memory was better than mine's been for years, and he still lived alone. Managed very well, too.''

"I suppose his neighbors helped.''

"Hah! He was the one who helped them. Not that he had many close neighbors; he lived out in the country. But he still drove, the last I knew, and he'd go in to town for groceries and bring some back for the woman next door if she was too busy to go for herself—that kind of thing. It's just like him to give me a last, nice little surprise, and I feel guilty as anything for not having kept in closer touch with him.''

"Well, then, you'll want to comply with his last request, won't you?'' Alan squeezed my hand and pretended not to notice the tear I had to wipe from my cheek.

"Well—I know it's ridiculously short notice, but—you would go with me, wouldn't you? You're not off on some international jaunt or other?"

For Alan, though he retired some time ago as chief constable of Belleshire, is still asked to contribute his expertise to police forces all over what used to be the British Empire, and I never knew for certain when he'd be hopping off to Africa or India or wherever.

"My dear, I am entirely at your disposal. Let's plan to stay on a bit after you've dealt with your business—at our own expense, of course—and make it a holiday. You write back to this solicitor or whatever she is, and tell her you're coming."

I barely heard him. "Alan." I stopped, groping after an elusive thought, and he looked at me quizzically. "Why do you suppose he wanted me to come back? I don't understand it. If he'd wanted to see me about something—though I can't imagine what—he'd have written, or phoned. But this way, making me come home after he's dead—it's odd. Bizarre. Almost—ghoulish." I shivered.

"Calm down, darling. He probably just wanted to give you a little treat, and chose this way of doing it so that you weren't likely to refuse."

"It's not like him," I insisted. "He was always generous, but never manipulative. He was full of good advice when someone needed it, but he never tried to make anyone take it. This is out of character. I'm not really sure I like it, after all."

"You're speculating ahead of your data, my dear. Sherlock Holmes warned us about that. Doubtless all will be made clear when we get there."

I'd never before organized an international journey on a few days' notice, but between the two of us, we managed. Alan bought our tickets at the exorbitant rates charged last-minute fliers. I took a leave of absence from my volunteer job at the Cathedral Bookshop and arranged with our next-door neighbor to look after the cats. And a sunny Wednesday afternoon in late September found us standing, somewhat stiff and tired, in the international terminal at Chicago's O'Hare Airport.

Alan yawned and dragged a hand across his cheek. "I could do with a shave."

"I could do with a nap."

In the end, after Alan had picked up the rental car and driven cautiously to our hotel, he thought of a better way to spend an hour or two. Afterward, relaxed and rejuvenated, we had a leisurely dinner and fell into bed.

I woke well before dawn the next morning and lay quietly, trying not to wake Alan. Something about his breathing, though, seemed a little too quiet.

"Alan," I whispered, "are you awake?"

"For the past hour, love. I didn't want to disturb you."

I sat up on one elbow. "Are you hungry?"

"Not particularly."

"Then let's go! The coffee shop here won't be open yet, but we can eat on the road. I know a place in South Bend—the food's wonderful, though you won't like the coffee."

"Happy to be home, are you?" He swung his feet out of bed and headed for the bathroom.

"Oh, Alan, I hadn't realized how much I wanted to show you! You can have the shower first, but hurry up!"

I drove. We were early enough to escape Chicago's horrendous rush-hour traffic, and a little over two hours later we were digging into an enormous breakfast at a pancake house in South Bend.

"You're English, aren't you?" The waitress smiled as she poured us a second cup of the sort of coffee my family used to call "damaged water." "I can tell by your accents."

Accents, plural? I gave Alan a shocked look. He patted my hand. "I'm English. My wife is American."

"Yeah? You sound just alike to me. Can I get you anything else?"

"Just the bill, please."

"Here you go. You pay up front. Have a nice day."

"Alan, I don't sound English!" I said indignantly, once we were back in the car.

"Not to me, love, but I expect you do to her. You can't expect to spend three years in a country and not absorb some of its influence. Careful!"

I swerved back to my side of the road and tried to ignore the angry shouts from the other driver. Clearly I had some adjustments to make.

Cincinnati is the closest major airport to my hometown in southern Indiana, but we'd chosen to fly into Chicago. The fare was a good deal cheaper, for one thing, and besides, I wanted to show Alan lots of my home state. So we meandered south from South Bend through lush farming country, acres of golden cornfields and green-yellow soybeans. Leaves were just beginning to turn in the northern part of the state. Here and there we saw a sumac hedge blazing with red and orange, a maple beginning to turn yellow. With the rising of the sun the day had turned almost hot. The cloudless sky was an intense shade of blue that I have seen only in the Midwest.

I fumbled for the air-conditioning controls and sighed

with contentment. Alan looked out the window and smiled in agreement.

We stayed off the interstates. Superhighways are great for getting places in a hurry, but if you want to see anything, slower roads win hands down. So we went through Indianapolis, rather than around. The traffic gave us plenty of time to see the Circle and the State-house and the various monuments and, it must be ad-mitted, the seamier aspects of town as well. We stopped in Columbus, just a little way south, to have some lunch and walk off too much driving, enjoying the famous, varied architecture of the town. Alan had to pull me back to the curb as I crossed one street; I'd looked the wrong direction for traffic and nearly gotten run over.

It was only a short drive then, along a narrow state highway, to Hillsburg.

We'd booked our hotel room from England and had been warned that we had to make other arrangements after a few days. "That next weekend's a home game," the desk clerk had said. I'd had to explain to Alan.

"Football. Our kind, not soccer. The sine qua non of American college life in the fall. *And* we're playing No-tre Dame. They haven't had a really good team for a couple of seasons, but they're still a legend in college football, and beating them would make the whole town happy all year. There won't be a hotel room for miles around that weekend, but we can either take off for a few days, or stay with one of my friends. I didn't like to impose on anyone for two or three weeks, but there are a lot of people who'd be glad to put us up for a weekend. Unless you'd rather just get away from all the crowds and hullabaloo."

"I want to see the football game," Alan had said firmly.

My mouth had gaped. Neither of us has much interest in sports.

"I like to learn," he'd explained. "I've never seen American football, and I understand it's part of the culture."

"I don't know that culture is exactly the word, but I'll see if I can get tickets."

It had felt odd, dickering by international telephone with box office personnel who'd never heard of me or Frank, when Frank, as faculty, used to be offered season tickets automatically. And it felt odd now to be hunting for a hotel in the town where I'd lived all my life. The hotel was new and I had trouble finding it, peering at street signs, looking for landmarks that seemed to have moved.

"Alan, I must have gotten turned around somehow. There ought to be a beautiful old bank on this corner."

The corner held an ugly new drugstore with a spacious parking lot. Alan looked at the old street map I'd found buried in a box back in England and said only, "No, this must be the place. Turn right."

We checked in and unpacked, rather silently.

"Pleasant room," Alan said.

"Yes." I folded underwear into a drawer.

"Tired, darling?"

"A little. It was a long drive." I bit my lip and turned away. Tears were trying to escape from the corners of my eyes.

Alan is a perceptive man. His natural powers of observation have been sharpened by years of training and experience as a policeman. He is also keenly sensitive. He said nothing more, but whistled as he hung up his clothes and arranged his shaving things to his liking in the bathroom.

I had planned to take him on a tour of the town and the university as soon as we arrived, but I was tired. Jet lag and a long drive and—well, that was enough, for goodness' sake. Undoubtedly weariness was responsible for the tears.

"I think I'll take a little nap."

"Good idea." Alan's tone was determinedly cheerful. "If you don't mind, I think I'll walk a little and orient myself."

"Fine."

I didn't want him to go, and he knew it, but after he'd left, I realized I was glad he was gone. I could cry if I wanted to, and I did.

I'd thought I was coming home. Why did everything seem so foreign?

MY APPOINTMENT with the lawyer was the next morning, Friday. For moral support, I put on one of my best-looking suits, a string of very nice pearls, and a soft velvet hat that packs well and flatters my gray hair.

"Do you want me to come with you, love?" Alan's hand paused over a selection of ties.

Even Alan was behaving oddly. "Of course I want you to come!"

"Sorry, darling. I seem to feel just a trifle out of place here. Slightly de trop."

I smiled somewhat grimly. "Not half as much as I do, I'll bet. And I'm not moving a step away from this hotel without you."

"Well, then." He chose a sober navy blue tie, presumably suitable for a lawyer's office, knotted it, donned a blazer, and held out his arm. I clung to it all the way out the lobby door.

"Do you want me to drive, as well?"

"I'm not sure which of us is the worse driver in this country, to tell the truth. I used to be really good, too! Let's just walk. It's not far, and my head needs clearing."

It was another lovely day. Our hotel was on one side of the Randolph University campus, the lawyer's office on the other, so it seemed natural to cut across. There were small changes that I, with heightened sensitivity, noted and resented. "That's a new wall. And what on earth have they done to the Bryant Building? Good grief, it's got a whole new wing! And double-ugly, too."

We dodged hurrying students.

"They, at least, haven't changed a bit. Except they look a little scruffier."

"That," Alan pronounced gravely, "is an inexorable law of nature."

The sun was warm. So was my suit. By the time we reached the office, I was grateful for the air-conditioning. I was, I told myself firmly, sweating only because of the heat.

"You're not nervous, are you, darling?" Alan spoke in an undertone.

"Of course not? Why should I be nervous?"

He smiled and clasped my hand.

Ms. Carmichael kept us waiting for only a moment or two before meeting us in a rather austere conference room.

"Sorry. I had a phone call at just the wrong moment." She shook hands with us. She was an attractive woman in her early forties, dressed with a minimum of feminine touches and very much all business in manner. "It's a pleasure to meet you, Mrs. Nesbitt. I've heard a lot about you and Professor Martin. I'm sorry for the occasion that brought you here, however. Dr. Cassidy was a fine man and a fine teacher.''

"You studied with him?''

"One class only, early in my undergraduate career. It was the last year he taught, I believe. He was in his seventies and made us all run to keep up with him. We would have done anything for him. And this must be your husband?''

"Alan Nesbitt, yes. And I don't actually use his name. I prefer Dorothy Martin.''

"I can understand that,'' she said, and grimaced, suddenly looking more human. "I took back my own name after my divorce.''

Alan and I exchanged looks. My choice of name had nothing to do with feelings about my marriage. "Yes, well. I suppose you'll want to see some identification? I brought my passport.''

"That's fine.'' She studied it, carefully comparing the photo with my face, and handed it back. "Well, that's that. Not that I was in any real doubt. You're exactly the way everybody described you.''

She was looking at my hat. I grinned. "I guess I'm pretty old-fashioned, but I *like* hats.''

"And they suit you. Now, I don't want to delay you, Mrs. Martin. I have your check prepared.'' She opened a slim manila folder on the table. "If you'll just sign the receipt—that's fine. You won't forget to send me your expenses, will you? And, finally, here is something I was directed by Dr. Cassidy to give you.''

She handed me two envelopes, one with a check showing through the cellophane window. The other was a stiff, heavy envelope. The flap was not only gummed down but sealed with a blob of wax. I studied it, suddenly nervous again.

"I'm sure you'll want to read your letter, if it is a letter, in privacy, and I have another appointment. Here's a letter opener. If you'll excuse me? Please take all the time you like. Can you find your own way out?"

I muttered something, Alan stood politely, and the young woman left the room, closing the door behind us.

"Alan, I don't like it!" I whispered. "The letter from beyond the grave. It feels spooky."

"My dear, I don't know why you're making so much of this." His normal tone of voice lowered the emotional temperature. "There are no doubt some things the professor wanted you to know, and perhaps he didn't trust international mail. An opinion that I must say I share."

"But why did he seal it so elaborately, then? Why did he seal it at all? I can't imagine anything he would have to say to me that would be as private as all that."

"Hmmm. That is perhaps a trifle odd, though some people have an exaggerated sense of privacy." Alan took the envelope from me and examined it carefully. "Well, it doesn't look as though the seals have been tampered with."

"Why should they be?" I demanded.

"I haven't any idea, except that when someone takes such precautions, it's usually because he expects some hanky-panky. Just in case, love, why don't you open it at the bottom?"

I looked at him sharply, but picked up the paper knife and slit the bottom of the envelope.

The enclosure was a single sheet of paper, again thick and heavy and expensive. "I don't understand this stationery, either. Kevin lived very simply. He was never ostentatious about things like stationery."

"More of the privacy concern, perhaps. I'd defy anybody to read that through the envelope, even held up to the strongest light.''

The paper was covered on both sides with the shaky handwriting of the very old. I spread it flat on the table so Alan and I could read it together.

Dear Dorothy,
By the time you read this, I'll be gone. We both know death isn't the end, and I'll see you again, though I trust not for some time, as time is counted on your side of the great divide. I wish you a long and happy life.

There is, however, one thing I wish you to do for me, which is why I have brought you here in this melodramatic way. It is a matter, I suppose, of shutting the barn door after the horse is stolen. I have tried to get in touch with you, but the idiots in the phone company claimed they didn't have your number, and you never replied to my letter.

"Alan, I never got a letter!"
Alan was reading ahead. He didn't respond.

You see, I have heard about your exploits as an amateur detective. You must be very careful

—this was underlined three times—

and say nothing to anyone, because this is a small town, and it could be almost anyone—my doctor, my lawyer, the police chief, one of my friends, even my own family, however painful it is to believe such a thing.

"What *is* he talking about?"

"Read on," said Alan, his voice grim. I looked up at him in surprise and then turned back to the letter.

You see, my dear, someone is trying to kill me. When you read this, they will have succeeded. There is little I can do. I hate to admit it, but I am too old and too frail to pursue an unknown enemy myself. I have no concrete evidence to take to the police, even if I could be sure the police were to be trusted. No, my murderer, or murderers, will succeed. It is not a great tragedy, not at my age, but it makes me angry. I would prefer to live out my life to the span God intended. Furthermore, I believe in justice. No one should be able to kill without retribution. I want you to find my murderer.

I repeat that you must be careful, but I have every confidence in you. You have done some remarkable things in the past, and with that Scotland Yard husband of yours to help, I know you will not fail me.

All my love, Kevin

TWO

We looked at each other in naked shock. "But—but—"

"Shh!" Alan's hiss was short and very quiet. "Let's get out of here. And try to act nonchalant." He put the letter back in its envelope and tucked it into his breast pocket before opening the door.

"It was certainly kind of your friend to remember you with such a nice note," he said in a crisp, carrying voice as we went through the outer office.

"Umm—yes, he was that kind of person." I bared my teeth in an imitation smile at the receptionist, who smiled in return and wished us a nice day.

"*Alan,*" I whispered urgently when we got outside.

"Yes, it certainly *is* a beautiful day," he replied with a brilliant smile. "Shall we take a stroll through the university?" He gripped my hand. "*Wait. No one will notice us on the paths.*"

He chatted inconsequentially until we were well inside the campus boundaries, and I exploded. "Alan, I *have* to talk about it!"

"I know. We should have relative privacy now. The students have their own concerns."

"Then let's sit somewhere. There's a bench."

"Don't look so grim," he warned.

"Look, I'm not Sarah Bernhardt! If anyone comes

near, we're talking about the death of an old friend, and
one I might have prevented. Of course I look grim!''

We settled. There was so much to say, I didn't know
where to start.

Alan broke the silence. ''You're feeling guilty, aren't
you?''

''Guilty and incredulous at the same time. If only we
hadn't changed the phone listing to your name. If only
that letter he sent hadn't gone astray! And yet—Alan, I
don't know how to take it. It's entirely unbelievable,
really. You're taking it seriously, though, or you
wouldn't have insisted on all the cloak-and-dagger
stuff.''

''A policeman learns to be careful. If there's the
slightest possibility that Professor Cassidy was right, we
can't take any chances. I admit that I remain highly
skeptical. The man died of pneumonia, didn't he?''

''That's what the letter said—the one from Ms. Carmichael.''

''Are we talking here about biological murder? The
deliberate introduction of a virus or bacillus into the professor's environment?''

Alan's tone was carefully neutral, but I flared up.

''How do I know what we're talking about? It's all
obviously impossible! That's the stuff of Golden Age
fiction, people going around planting germs or untrace-
able poisons all over the place.'' I thought about Agatha
Christie's *Easy to Kill* and *The Pale Horse*—two wonderful books, but nobody ever claimed that their plots
were highly realistic.

''Yes, you're right.'' There was an awkward pause.
''Dorothy, try to set aside your feelings for a moment
and tell me what sort of man Professor Cassidy was,
besides a kind one and a good friend. Did he have a

lively imagination? No," he said, raising his hand as I glared at him, "I'm not implying anything. We have to deal with facts, my dear, and your friend's character and personality are part of the facts. I know you loved him, and I know he was still a thoughtful old bloke."

"How do you know that?"

"He got you here as quickly as he could. Wanted the trail to be as warm as possible. That implies a certain amount of consideration as well as intelligence."

My annoyance was swallowed up in admiration for a neat piece of deduction. "Yes, he was considerate, and very intelligent."

I thought about Kevin, trying to obey Alan and be objective. "First and foremost, he was a scientist," I said finally. "A very, very good one. He helped, back in the fifties, to develop some wonderful new antibiotics. He made a great deal of money from the patents, in fact. So he had the kind of imagination it took to devise experiments and draw inspired conclusions from the results. But he also had the kind of absolutely logical mind that would never, ever jump to conclusions."

"Go on. Tell me about his family, his friends."

"He had very little family. A sister and a brother who both died some time ago, and their children and grandchildren. No one closer. He never married. It wasn't that he was cold or distant—quite the contrary. You already know how wonderful he was to me, but it wasn't just me. He enjoyed everyone's company and loved to flirt with pretty women. But he was truly dedicated to his work as a microbiologist. He told me once that everything in his life was secondary to that. He never felt it would be fair to neglect a wife when some experiment required his constant presence in the lab.

"But he had piles of friends, mostly among the students and alumni and faculty. When he wasn't buried in microbes, he was a fine, caring teacher. Everyone on campus loved him, and that's pretty unusual in a university, believe me. The petty jealousies can create vicious infighting. But Kevin was above campus politics. He never took sides, but he used to show up at faculty parties and make a point of trying to reconcile combatants. The remarkable thing is that he sometimes succeeded!''

Alan groaned. "The universally beloved victim. The stuff of fiction, indeed!''

"Well, I can't help it. You did ask.''

"I did. You mentioned one promising detail, however. He was a wealthy man?''

"Hmm. He certainly was at one time. His work on antibiotics came before the pharmaceutical houses began sponsoring all the research, so he owned his patents outright, and they brought in tons of money.''

"What's 'tons'?''

"Oh, hundreds and hundreds of thousands. Maybe even a million or two. But of course as the germs got smarter and the antibiotics began to lose their effectiveness, the money dried up.''

"But he must surely have invested it. Or did he spend it all in riotous living?''

"Not Kevin! He lived in a log cabin that he built himself, out in the woods; he liked the simple life. He invested some of the money, of course, but he also poured a lot back into research. Randolph University isn't exactly poor, but it isn't Harvard, and it can't afford to have really superbly equipped labs. Anyway it couldn't back then. Kevin bought equipment and supplies and paid his assistants out of his own money. All in all, I wouldn't think he could really be a wealthy man by now. And then there were the loans.''

Alan perked up. "Loans?"

"Well, he called them that. He was always on the lookout for students or friends who were in a bind for money, and he'd ask if they could use a small loan. People almost never came to him. He was so sweet, nobody liked to take advantage, and then he didn't exactly advertise himself as a bank. But if a grad student's wife had a baby and they couldn't make ends meet, or a part-time faculty member didn't have work one semester, or somebody needed to go to a conference and couldn't afford it, there was Kevin, ready with a handout.''

"I thought you said they were loans."

"In name only. Kevin always drew up promissory notes. I think he had stacks of them printed, just ready to fill in the names and dates and amounts. But he never expected anybody to pay the money back, really. It was just so people's pride wouldn't be hurt.''

"So nobody would kill him to avoid paying back a large sum of money.''

"Heavens, no! Some people did pay him back, of course. Frank and I did. He helped finance our first sabbatical in England, you see. But he never made any demands. I think he forgot about most of the deals. And very few of them were for large amounts, anyway. At least, so far as I know. The whole thing was kind of a secret, you see. A conspiracy of silence among Kevin's friends and the people he helped, so he wouldn't end up with beggars on his doorstep.''

Alan ran a hand down the back of his head in a familiar gesture of frustration. "Yes. Well, we haven't exhausted all the possibilities, but on the face of it he doesn't appear to be a likely murder victim.''

"No. But—the letter—''

"Yes. The letter.''

We were back to that charged silence.

"Alan, honestly, he wasn't at all likely to make up something stupid.''

"I hate to say this, love, but you last saw him—when?''

"I know, I know. Over three years ago. And yes, he was very, very old. And old people do lose their marbles and get paranoid and all the rest of it. But his last Christmas card was perfectly sane and lucid. And even though the content of the sealed letter was pretty weird, the tone was quite reasonable. Don't you think?''

Alan stood up and sighed. "What I think is that we don't know anything like enough to make any judgment. And I also think—no, I *know*—that our holiday is a total loss until we learn enough to dismiss the question.''

I stood, too, and we began to walk slowly to the edge of the campus. "Then you don't believe it?''

"Not yet, no. But I'm keeping an open mind until we have some hard facts.''

I breathed a sigh of relief, careful to keep it inaudible. "Alan, I was so afraid you were going to say we ought to just forget about it. And I couldn't have done that.''

He tucked my hand under his arm. "My dear, I would have liked to say just that. I dislike the idea of your becoming involved in anything that even might bring you into danger. But we made a pact quite some time ago, didn't we? I promised to curb my protective instincts if you would promise to use reasonable caution.

"Besides,'' he added, "I was a policeman for too

many years not to be intrigued. I, too, want to get to the bottom of this.''

"Then we need a plan of action," I said eagerly.

"Pencil and paper. Back to the hotel, Sherlock."

The hotel room was a typical one, clean, bland, anonymous. King-size bed with an ultra-firm mattress I hated, bedside table, desk, chest of drawers, television cabinet, round table with two chairs. The only available paper, besides that provided for hygienic purposes, was a telephone pad about three inches wide. Alan picked it up with a look of distaste and sat down with me at the table.

"What do we need to know?" he began.

"Everything."

"Right. But we have to start somewhere."

"Where would you start, if we were at—if we were in England?"

"With the SOCOs' report. If, of course, a crime had been reported and scene of crime officers had been dispatched."

"Well, that doesn't get us much of anywhere here, does it? I mean, there was no apparent crime, and I very much doubt if the police were even involved."

"But we don't know that, do we? We know nothing whatever about the circumstances of the professor's death."

"That's true. Maybe that's the first thing to ask about."

"And whom," said Alan, "do you plan to ask?"

"His doctor, his neighbors—oh."

"Exactly. 'Say nothing to anyone.'"

"But then how on earth…?"

Alan made a face. "It does appear, doesn't it, that your friend has set you an impossible task. You're to investigate a crime that may not be a crime, and without talking to anyone.''

I got up from the table and began to pace the limited confines of the room.

''He didn't say I couldn't talk to anyone. Or he didn't mean that. He meant I mustn't ask dangerous questions. Alan, this is my hometown. I know lots of people. It would be more suspicious if I *didn't* talk to them, and what could be more natural than to inquire into Kevin's death? I'll just have to play it cool and not let it look as though I'm prying into anything specific.''

He looked dubious.

''No, I can do this. We already have one invitation to dinner, you know, and as soon as word gets out that I'm in town, there'll be more. There'll be lots of chances to talk.''

The phone rang. I was closest. ''Hello?''

''Is this Dorothy Martin? Could you hold, please, for Dr. Foley?''

The phone went dead for a moment. ''His doctor,'' I mouthed at Alan. ''And mine. He and his wife have been friends for years.''

''Dorothy?'' The phone came back to life.

''Nice to hear from you, Doc.''

There was a brief pause. ''You don't sound quite like yourself.''

''Oh, Doc, I'm just me, the same old person. *Don't* tell me I sound English!''

A chuckle. ''Okay, I won't. I heard you were in town, and I called to see if you can come to dinner tonight. Short notice, but it just happens I have no babies due and nobody in the hospital with anything critical, so unless somebody has a heart attack or an appendix takes a notion to get fussy, I should be free. A doctor has to seize the moment, you know. And I think Peggy has some salmon all ready for the grill."

"Ah, the salmon clinches it. We'd love to. What time?"

"Eightish? I've got a long day here."

"Eightish it is. Keep your fingers crossed about those hearts and appendixes. Appendices?"

He chuckled again and hung up. I looked at Alan with, I'm afraid, a smug expression. "That's one down."

He began to laugh. "And the other dinner invitation? I presume it's from the attorney, the chief of police, or the professor's next of kin?"

"Actually, no. Frank's old dean and his wife. So they fall into the other category Kevin mentioned, his friends. Not that everyone in town wasn't his friend."

I fell silent and bit my lip. Alan's eyes held sympathy.

"This is a trifle difficult for you, isn't it, love?"

"More than a trifle. I'm so confused, Alan. It seems so impossible that anyone could have murdered Kevin. He was a genuinely good man, and everyone who knew him really did love him. He never harmed a living soul. In fact, those antibiotics of his saved thousands of lives, maybe millions. And yet—and yet he was also an extremely intelligent and supremely logical man, and he was convinced someone was trying to kill him. So convinced that he tried to enlist my help, and when he couldn't, he commissioned me to catch his murderer. I have to accept that commission, no matter how remote the possibility that Kevin was right. I owe it to him." My lip trembled a little.

"Of course you do." Alan spoke briskly. He knows how to deal with my moods. "So I suggest we go out and find ourselves some lunch, and then buy a proper notebook and begin to lay out procedure. We will be able to find a notebook in some shop or other, I trust?''

I giggled, as he meant me to. ''Alan, this is a college town. We'll trip over them! All emblazoned in gold with the seal of Randolph University. We'll go to the biggest bookstore the minute we've finished eating. Right now I'm going to show you where to find the best stromboli sandwich in the world.''

THREE

AN HOUR LATER, replete with sausage, peppers, onions, tomato sauce, mozzarella, and entirely too much bread, we repaired to Howard's, the huge bookstore that had served the needs of Randolph University for well over a hundred years. I had to drag Alan away from the display of college souvenirs.

"They're so gaudy, so brash, so—"

"Is tacky the word you're looking for?"

"No, indeed! Actually they're quite well made, for the most part, and certainly they're colorful. But why the tiger? Surely there are no tigers in this part of the world."

I laughed. "Only in the zoos. No, you see, John Randolph was a very wealthy young man in the early nineteenth century. He went on a grand tour that was even grander than most, including both Europe *and* points East. He apparently fell in love with tigers in India, and the passion never deserted him. So later on, when he decided to perpetuate his name by founding a college, he insisted that the architect feature decorative tigers. I'll show you the original ones on the Administration Building. And later trustees kept up the tradition, so now they're all over the place, on gateposts and benches and wherever. There even used to be a topiary one over by the horticulture building, though I don't know if they've kept it clipped. It was only natural that a tiger become the mascot; it's a nice, fierce symbol for the football team. Come on, we're looking for a notebook.''

There was, of course, a tiger's head on the spiral notebooks. I bought four of them, thick ones with subject dividers. I have a thing for spiral notebooks, and I can't find the kind I like in England. Alan drifted back to the souvenirs. When we finally left the store he had acquired five tiger sweatshirts in various sizes for his grandchildren and one for each of us, a tiger tie, tiger bookends, and a really splendid stuffed tiger at a really inflated price. I had to carry the stuffed one.

"Remind me never to take you shopping again." I shifted my awkward burden. A striped tail poked me in the eye.

"Oh, but you will, the next time you visit a mystery bookshop. You can't carry fifty or sixty books yourself."

I shut up.

Our purchases—mostly Alan's purchases—took up a good deal of space in our hotel room. The sweatshirts would fit on the closet shelf if we removed the extra pillows, but they kept cascading to the floor in their plastic bags. I finally moved my nightgowns and underwear to the shelf and stuffed the shirts, with some difficulty, into the drawer. The tiger went on top of the television cabinet, where its snarl intimidated us. I made a face, and Alan looked a little abashed.

"We may perhaps need to post a few things back to Sherebury?" he suggested. "Sorry for the clutter, darling. I've not been in the habit of acquiring barnacles on my travels, not on this scale, at any rate."

I took pity. "The first time I went to England I bought everything in sight. We'll send things back, of course, but we might as well wait a while. As you just reminded me, there's a mystery bookstore in town, and I can't go back to England without hitting it. Books are a lot cheaper over here.''

I shoved the tie box and the bookends to one side of the table and sat down with one of my bright, shiny new notebooks. All that virgin paper was revving my mind.

"Now. First of all, we need to find out exactly how Kevin died. When, where, how long he was sick—all that.''

"Also who was with him when he died and immediately before he became ill.''

"Yes, very good. I'd forgotten about that. That'll be a little harder, though.'' I wrote:

1. Circumstances of death
2. Who was present?

"Next—what's next, Alan?''

"The classic triad: means, motive, opportunity. We can't deal with means or opportunity until we know the precise cause of death, so motive seems a logical pursuit at this stage. Though it's the weakest link in making a case, you know.''

"I know, but it's always been my favorite. Means and opportunity are more police concerns, forensic evidence kinds of things. An amateur can find out a lot about motive just by talking to people.''

"You're probably right. So shall we approach the specific people the professor—''

"Call him Kevin. He'd want you to if he were alive.''

"Very well, the people Kevin mentioned specifically?''

"I think we have to, you know. There had to be a

reason he cited them in particular. He might not have known who was trying to get rid of him, but those people came to mind when he was writing a very important letter. Subconsciously, maybe, he had some reason for suspecting them.''

''Right. Then the next thing on your list ought to be a schedule of interviews.''

Obediently, I wrote:

3. Interviews
   a. Doctor

''That's tonight, but I put him down so there's a place to write the report.''

If Alan smiled he hid it very well. I continued:

   b. Police Chief
   c. Attorney
   d. Kevin's family?

''I can't put down 'friends,''' I said as Alan looked upside down at what I'd written. ''We'd be here for months.''

''The query after family?''

''I'm not sure which ones live here. He didn't—it's funny, Alan, now that I think about it, but he never talked about his family much.''

''Problems?''

''I don't know. It's worth following up, though.'' I added an exclamation point to the ''family'' entry and then stared into space, tapping my pen on the notebook.

''Idea?''

"I don't know. I'm just thinking…. Alan, what made Kevin think someone was trying to kill him?"

"Well, I think we've agreed, as a working hypothesis, that he wasn't going dotty."

"Yes, that's what I mean. If he was all there, and I'll swear he was, at least as late as last December, then there must have been something concrete to make him suspicious. In fact, Alan, there must have been attempts that didn't succeed."

"Of course!" Alan smacked the table. "Other illnesses—accidents—"

"Funny things sent to him in the mail."

"And they must all have been cleverly done, so that he had no idea who the villain might be."

"And so there was nothing to take to the police. But he wasn't quite clever enough, was he—or she, whoever it was? Because Kevin's suspicions were aroused, and he didn't die."

"But he did die, Dorothy. In the end, he did die."

That sobered me. I have a tendency to view an investigation as a puzzle, a game. But we were dealing here with a man I had loved like a father, who had possibly been murdered. I tried to think logically. "It could, just barely, have been coincidence. Attempts at murder and then, at the end, an old man carried away by pneumonia. The murderer must have been delighted."

"If there were other incidents. If there was a murderer, or a would-be murderer. If we're not inventing the whole scenario."

"You're right. All we have to go on at the moment is what Kevin said. We've got to start collecting evidence."

"And we do need to heed Kevin's advice and be very, very careful, Dorothy. Because if there is a murderer, he's been successful. He's got away with it. He'll feel he can kill again.''

I set my jaw and added to my list:

4. What happened to make Kevin suspicious?

Then I closed the notebook and buried it under the sweatshirts in the drawer. ''Okay. We'll defer any more action and speculation till we've talked to Dr. Foley and know a little more. Now shall we go get some exercise in this beautiful weather, or shall we take a nap? I think I'm still a little jet-lagged.''

''Is there any reason,'' asked my loving husband, a wicked expression in his blue eyes, ''why we couldn't combine exercise with a nap?''

WE DRESSED INFORMALLY for dinner with the Foleys. The doctor, I knew, would be tired after a day beginning with six o'clock hospital rounds and ending after seven with phone calls to patients. He wouldn't dress up. And Peggy, the kind of woman who looks terrific in anything, might be wearing blue jeans or a Chanel suit; you never knew. So I put on nice slacks and a favorite sweater, and I even let Alan wear his new sweatshirt over his shirt. ''It'll be too warm for you in the house. You know Americans and central heating. And it'll leave fuzz all over your shirt when you take it off. But you look nice in it.''

He did. It was dark green, the better to set off orange tiger stripes, and it was big, the better to enclose Alan's sturdy physique. He looked very, very solid and dependable, and I had to give him a hug.

The Foleys live out in the country, not far from

Kevin's little house. Their house was light-years removed in style, though.

"Good heavens," said Alan quietly as I maneuvered the car around the curved drive and parked in front of the door.

"I know. Peggy inherited it from her parents, along with a good deal of money, and Doc hasn't done at all badly in his practice."

"It looks like Tara. Only larger."

"They're not like that, though. Unassuming people. You'll like them. Oh, and call him Doc. Everybody does, even his wife."

Alan still sat there. "Dorothy, you haven't, I trust, forgotten that these charming people may be murder suspects?"

I took my hand off the door handle. "Oh. I *had* forgotten. I was just thinking about seeing old friends, and incidentally picking up information. But Kevin did say... Alan, I'm not sure I like this."

"Goes with the territory, my dear." He got out of the car and came around to help me out. "Shall we?"

Arm in arm, we rang the bell of the lion's den.

I COULDN'T RAISE the subject until after dinner. The food was too good to neglect, for one thing, and Doc, who is an enormous man, did full credit to it. And both Peggy and Doc kept us talking, between bites, about life in England. Alan hit it off immediately with both of them, to my relief. It isn't always a good idea to tell someone in advance that he'll like someone else, but Alan is an amiable sort of man, and the Foleys are both entertaining people. Alan told a fish story, Doc topped it with a hospital story, and we repaired to the living room for our coffee aching a little with laughter.

"Decaf," said Peggy, passing a cup to me. "Doc insists. Me, I like the real stuff, but I've found a good brand of decaf, and I hope it's okay. Dorothy, I can't tell you how glad I am to see you again. I've missed you."

"I'm glad to be back, but sorry for the reason."

"Ain't it the truth? We were all really broken up about Kevin. Somehow we expected him to go on forever."

"No reason why he shouldn't have," said Doc gruffly. "Not forever, maybe, but a good while longer. I've got patients of fifty who aren't anything like as healthy as he was at ninety-six. I thought for sure he'd live to a hundred, at least. Oh, he was getting a little frail. I kept after him to get some help in that little house of his. I didn't want him chopping wood anymore, or plowing his garden. I think he was about to give in, too, but——" He spread his hands.

"Just how did he die, Doc?" I said, hoping my voice didn't sound as tense as I felt. "I really haven't heard any of the details."

"And I can't give them to you."

"But——oh, medical ethics, I suppose." I was a little hurt. Doc had never been one to stand on ceremony with me.

"Come on, Dorothy. You know me better than that, and besides, the man's dead. Can't hurt him now. No, it's just that I wasn't there." He settled back more comfortably in a massive leather chair that would have suited Nero Wolfe. "You know I don't go away much——"

Peggy snorted. "Much! Three or four real vacations in forty years!"

Doc just grinned at her. "But there was an AMA convention up in Minneapolis, and Peggy's folks are from those parts, so she talked me into going. Waste of time, most of it. One or two useful seminars, maybe. Anyway, I left my practice with Jim Boland, decent young guy who has an office in the same building. He doesn't have a lot of patients yet, so I give him my overflow from time to time. Well, we fill in for each other, really. It's time I started thinking about who'll take over from me when I retire."

Peggy snorted again, but said nothing. I wasn't sure whether she was commenting on anyone's ability to take over from Doc or the unlikelihood of his ever consenting to retire.

"*Anyway,* I got back to find Kevin in the hospital with galloping pneumonia. We pumped him full of antibiotics and did everything possible, but his heart at ninety-six…" He sighed. "He died comfortably, Dorothy. Slipped into a coma and just didn't wake up. He was lucid almost to the end, and as serene as he always was."

"Did he—" I cleared my throat to try to get rid of the lump in it. "Did he know he was dying?"

Doc's eyes held pity. "He was a microbiologist, Dorothy. He fought it, fought it hard, but the last couple of days, he knew he'd lost the battle, and then he just accepted it." Doc seemed to have an obstruction in his throat, too. "He was a great man."

There were other questions I wanted to ask, but I knew I'd start bawling like a baby if I opened my mouth. Alan must have seen my chin quiver. He nodded reassuringly and addressed Doc.

"I'm sorry I'll never have the chance to know him. He sounds like a remarkable person. I suppose it was the usual pattern for someone his age—fell and broke his hip and contracted pneumonia?"

"Not this time. No broken bones. Anyway, his bones were strong as an ox's. Came from all that exercise he always got, and eating healthy. No, no telling how he got it, really."

"We had that freak cold spell just about then," Peggy put in. "Down in the fifties, Dorothy, forties one night. I can count on the fingers of one hand the number of times that's happened around here in August! And Kevin didn't have a furnace, you know, only that old woodstove."

"His woodstove isn't all that old," said Doc. "It's a modern Franklin stove, and Kevin had that cabin good and tight. He liked to be warm, the way old people do. Anyway, you don't get pneumonia from being cold. You get it from a virus, or a bacterium, depending. He must've picked up a bug somewhere, and then took too long to get to a doctor."

"Now, Doc, you're *not* going to start that again, are you?" Peggy shook her head. "He blames himself. Thinks if he'd been here, Kevin would've waltzed right in to the office when he first started to cough. It's just plain stupid! No, Doc, let me have my say. I've told you a dozen times: Kevin always did think he could take care of himself, and never went to see you till he was sick as a dog. Why, that time he fell down his front steps, he never even went in at all!"

I recovered my voice. "Fell down the steps?"

"Yes, Doc saw him limping down Main Street one day and asked him what happened. He said he'd sprained his ankle. And would you believe he wouldn't even let Doc X-ray it? Said he knew it wasn't broken, and an Ace bandage was all he needed."

"Good grief! What did he do, slip on an icy step?"

"No, it was in the spring," said Doc. "Just tripped,

I guess. That was when I started agitating for him to get some help in the house, but he wouldn't hear of it. Just said he was going to get new glasses so he wouldn't trip over his own feet like an old fool. Well, I couldn't force him to do anything, could I?''

He sounded a little defensive.

"It is difficult, isn't it?" said Alan tactfully. "We worry about the elderly and try to look after them, but they don't want to give up their independence, and one can understand, really. My own mother is a case in point." He went off into a rather rambling reminiscence that eventually turned the subject to cats and crocheting, and we finished the evening on a pleasant note.

But when Alan and I were driving back to the hotel, I said, "He fell down the steps."

"Yes. That's one accident. Do you suppose we'll find others?"

FOUR

THE NEXT MORNING we spent some time planning a strategy. First I got out the notebook and entered our meager discoveries:

1. Circumstances of death
   No broken bones. Died in hospital. Cause of pneumonia not known. Bug? Where had he been lately?
2. Who was present?
   Not Doc Foley, beforehand. Who was?

"We haven't gotten very far, have we?"

"Not very. But a little farther than we were. We know your doctor—whom I like very much, by the way—wasn't present immediately before Kevin became ill. We know it was a straightforward case of pneumonia. And we know Kevin had had at least one accident."

I sighed. "The trouble is, it points both ways. Plain old pneumonia—but a previous accident. Oh, but wait a minute, Alan! *Do* we know it was, as you put it, a straightforward illness? Doc didn't tell us he'd looked at X rays or anything. Maybe it was something else, some disease that looks like pneumonia but won't be cured by the antibiotics they usually use! Maybe—"

"Dorothy, I don't want to dampen your enthusiasm, but Dr. Foley strikes me as an extremely competent and caring physician. I doubt he would misdiagnose a case at this stage in his career, especially when the patient was a very old friend."

"Oh, you're probably right. Well, what's next, then?"

"I think we want to look into other accidents. Or perhaps 'incidents' would be a better word to use. Anything at all unusual that occurred in Kevin's life in the period shortly before his death."

"Golly, that could cover a lot of territory. How long before, do you think?"

"His letter to you wasn't dated, was it?"

"It's still in your coat pocket. Check."

He went to the closet and came back with the stiff envelope in his hand. "No," he said, taking the letter out and glancing at it. "No date." He put the letter back in the envelope and took the packet to the window, where he studied it very carefully in the strong light of a sunny morning. "I wish I had a magnifying glass," he muttered.

I fished my deluxe Swiss Army knife out of my purse, pulled up the minute magnifier, and handed the contraption to him.

He smiled, one of those superior male smiles that can be so infuriating. "Thank you, my dear, but I require something larger than my thumb. I seem to recall a glass amongst the university souvenirs; I'll buy one later. Meanwhile, do you think it would be as well to keep this document in the hotel safe?"

"Why? What do you suspect?"

"I told you before, I think like a policeman. The letter, in the wrong hands, could be dangerous. One tries to avoid danger. One also tries to preserve evidence. I don't suppose you have a larger envelope we could put it in?''

''As it happens, I do.'' I hauled it, too, out of my capacious handbag. ''I was saving receipts in it, for when we submit our expenses.''

''*If* we submit our expenses.''

''But, Alan—''

''The charming Ms. Carmichael could be our villain, you know.''

''Oh.''

''Meanwhile,'' he said, putting the smaller envelope in the larger one, ''back to our strategy. How are we to learn of Kevin's recent history, say for the past six months?''

I avoided looking at the envelope, which my lively imagination had endowed with all the aspects of a bomb, and pulled my thoughts together. ''Talk to his neighbors, I suppose. He doesn't have many, living where he does—did—but there are a few, and I think they all sort of looked out for him.''

''Do you know them?''

''Some of them, a little, or at least I used to. But I think they'll talk to me. Southern Indiana is a pretty friendly sort of place. And while we're out there we can look over his house, too. He almost never kept it locked, and there might be some evidence there.''

''Then think of a good excuse to talk to people, and let's go.''

I still hadn't come up with anything very convincing by the time we rolled up in front of Kevin's cabin. I'd gotten mildly lost on the way. The country roads in that part of Indiana can be confusing, and I'd called on Kevin only a few times during our long acquaintance, usually with Frank driving.

"It's quite nice, actually," said Alan in a surprised sort of voice as we extricated ourselves from the car with the little grunts that movement seems to elicit at our age.

"Well, of course. What were you expecting, Davy Crockett?"

"More or less, I suppose."

We stood arm in arm looking at Kevin's home.

It was set well back from the road, down a winding drive, in a little clearing. All around the house were oak and maple trees just beginning to put on their autumn dress. Now and then a leaf would drift down lazily through the golden dust motes to land amid the brilliant red and orange and lavender and white chrysanthemums of Kevin's flower garden.

The house, a snug bungalow, was made of pine logs, warm and golden in the sun. The windows and door hung straight and true. A couple of rocking chairs on the front porch welcomed visitors with soft cushions. Crisp red-checked curtains hung at the windows, which shone with cleanliness, even a month or more after Kevin had last been able to care for them. On one side of the house rose a fieldstone chimney, well built and in excellent repair, with a couple of cords of firewood neatly stacked nearby. At the back a sort of lean-to shed protruded. I didn't remember that part, but then I hadn't been out here in years.

There were a few weeds in the gardens, but the flowers bloomed riotously. Tomatoes and zucchini and acorn squash and kale and cabbage and brussel sprouts and cucumbers, along with chives and basil and oregano and dill and other herbs I couldn't name, grew in a profusion that would have provided Kevin with plenty of food to put up for the winter. From somewhere around back came the heady scent of Concord grapes, and an apple tree by the front porch was heavy with russet-and-green fruit.

"It's a friendly house," said Alan.

"It was."

"I suppose those are the steps he fell down." He pointed to the porch steps. "Odd. There's a handrail, and the whole affair looks quite sturdy."

"He took great pride in his house and always kept it in good repair. Oh, Alan!" I put my head against his chest and cried the first real tears I had shed since I had heard of Kevin's death.

"Feel better?" he said a few minutes later when I'd reached the sniffles-and-tissue stage.

I blew my nose.

"I suppose so. It was just the thought of this sweet house waiting for him, and the garden, and he'll never taste those grapes, or sit in front of another fire in his stove. That's what that nice chimney's for: the Franklin stove, not an open fire. Kevin was so proud of that stove, Alan. He installed it himself, very carefully so there was no danger of fire. It kept the whole place toasty warm. And it pleased him that he wasn't using up fossil fuels. He didn't even cut down live trees, mostly, just used the ones that were felled by storms, or else he culled saplings that didn't have enough light in the woods to grow properly."

I sniffled again. "He truly loved all creation, I think. His cats—oh, my word, Alan, I never thought about his cats! He always had a lot of them. I just hope—"

"You got no call to fret about them cats, ma'am."

We both whirled. There had been no sound to warn of anyone's approach.

"I wouldn't let no animal starve, 'specially the professor's. Them cats is safe with me." The voice was raspy and more than a little belligerent, and the man who'd come up behind us matched the voice. He was even bigger than Alan, but his weight ran to fat rather than muscle. His grizzled beard was long and unkempt. His checkered wool shirt, hanging over a capacious belly, was torn and dirty. He stood looking from one of us to the other, a rifle dangling casually from one hairy paw. The rifle pointed to the ground, but the giant's attitude clearly indicated that it might be raised at any moment.

"You got some business around here?"

I was struck dumb, but Alan nodded pleasantly, if a little warily. "Professor Cassidy was a great friend of my wife's. We came to see his house, by way of pilgrimage."

"Huh? Hey, where you from, anyways?"

"I'm from England. My wife was born and raised in Hillsburg."

The massive head turned my way. "Then how come you talk funny, too? I heard you when I come up."

I was getting tired of remarks about my accent. "I've lived away from here for several years. My name is Dorothy Martin, by the way. My husband—my late husband—was a professor, too. We used to come and visit Kevin now and then, but I don't believe we've ever met." I held out my hand. It was ignored.

"Y'know, I don't much like strangers comin' pokin' around. I kept an eye on the place when the professor was alive and I'm still keepin' an eye on it. Don't want nobody stealin' nothin'. He was a good man, the professor."

I wondered if it would help if I identified Alan as a retired policeman. I decided not.

In fact, I wasn't sure what to do. We certainly couldn't

go into the house with the self-appointed guardian there, nor even peer in the windows. And the giant was extremely intimidating. I looked helplessly at Alan.

He came through in style. "I'm sure all the professor's friends are very grateful to you, Mr.—I'm sorry, I didn't catch your name." He spoke very slowly and articulated very carefully.

"Jerry's the name. Pleased to meetcha." He shifted the rifle and squeezed Alan's hand. I saw the fleeting expression of pain cross Alan's face, but he managed not to wring his hand. I got the picture. He would shake Alan's hand, but not mine. That put me in *my* place!

"Mine's Alan. We've been worried, my wife and I, about Professor Cassidy's house, and of course his animals, but it's obvious you have everything under control. Though I don't suppose there's any danger, really. Certainly there can't be very much traffic in this out-of-the-way spot."

"Traffic? Ain't no traffic. This here driveway don't go no place."

"Sorry, I meant foot traffic. People coming to call—to visit."

"Mister, ain't nobody comin'," said the giant patiently. "Nobody comes to a man's house when he's dead. 'Cept you folks." The suspicion, which had abated, crept back into his voice.

"Of course. I seem to be very stupid today. What I meant to say was, did people come to see him before he became ill?"

"Not many, not no more. I been livin' over yonder"—he gestured vaguely with the rifle—"gettin' on for thirty years now. Used to be people comin' all the time, kids, other professors." He looked back at me; his gaze sharpened, focused on my bright orange linen hat.

"Sa-ay! I think mebbe I do remember you now. Are you the crazy woman who always used to show up in hats?"

I accepted the adjective. "That's me."

The giant looked at me critically. "You wasn't so fat then. And your hair wasn't gray."

I judged that it was not a moment to take offense. "Time is cruel, isn't it? How is it that I don't remember you at all?"

"Never let myself be seen. Just kept an eye on the comin's and goin's, that's all. The professor, he was good to me, and I reckon he trusted ever'body. Don't do to trust ever'body. I looked out for him. Hey, how come you want to know so much?"

Alan opened his mouth, but I poked him in the elbow. I was ready for this one.

"I moved away, you see, a few years ago when my husband died. I'd lost touch with Kevin. And now I feel guilty. I wanted to talk to the people who saw the most of him at the end, make sure he was well and happy— oh, I suppose just make sure there was nothing I could have done. I know it doesn't make sense, but he was good to me, too, Jerry. I loved him."

The bearded face split in what might have been a smile. The whiskers made it hard to tell. "Lady, you're mebbe all right after all. You want to know about the professor, you come with me. I can tell you anything you want to know. Come on, then!" he said impatiently.

He turned his back and stomped off. I looked at Alan. He raised his eyebrows fractionally, then shrugged and jerked his head.

We followed Jerry into the woods.

FIVE

ALAN'S EYEBROWS rose again, a little higher, when we reached our destination.

Jerry's home, though only a few yards away from Kevin's, was well hidden. It was a trailer. "Mobile home" didn't suit it at all. This was a 1950s-era trailer. Not that it would ever trail behind anything ever again. The tough, wiry vines of bindweed had knitted it firmly to the ground.

It was surrounded by junk. An old television and a front-loading washing machine leaned drunkenly against each other. Their two large, mismatched glass eyes stared out at us. Broken furniture, a bedspring, discarded cans and bottles, and several rusting hulks of cars sketched a sadly familiar scene of rural poverty. The only vehicle that looked to be in running condition was a motorcycle, an elderly but still mean-looking Harley Davidson. All in character.

The trailer itself, however, was not quite what one would expect. The concrete blocks for a doorstep, the sagging door, the torn screen, yes. But the body of the trailer—

"Surprised you, huh? The professor give me the paint. Nice 'n' bright, ain't it?"

It was. Jerry's home was painted a vivid glow-in-the-dark orange.

"I've never seen anything like it," I said with the utmost sincerity.

"It ain't the right kind of paint, the professor said. It'll wear off pretty soon. But he give me plenty, so's I can keep fixin' it. Kind of a memorial to him, like. Well, come on in."

I took a deep breath of what was likely to be the last fresh air I'd get for a while and followed the giant into his den, Alan behind me.

"You gotta bang the door." Jerry turned back and did just that. "It don't shut good. Got to fix that one of these days."

I wished he'd left it open. It was as dirty inside as I'd feared, and as odorous. The smell of stale food and unwashed human was no match for the pervasive smell of cat. The couch was covered with a fine collection of clothes, jumbled together with several weeks' worth of *TV Guide*s and the crumbs of a good many meals. Jerry scooped it all off and dumped it on the floor on top of a pizza box with a couple of dead slices still in it.

"Take a load off your feet. Want a beer?"

It still lacked an hour or so till noon. I shook my head, but Alan said, "Yes, thank you very much. My throat's quite dry. Dorothy will have one, too. She was only being polite."

"Alan!" I said in an undertone as Jerry rummaged in his refrigerator.

"I know, and you don't actually have to drink it, but I think we must accept his hospitality. If we refused beer he might offer something else, and at least beer comes in clean cans or bottles."

Jerry gave us our beers, took a long pull of his own, and sat himself down in a battered recliner.

"Where are the cats?" I asked brightly, as I inhaled a strong reminder of their presence.

"Around. They don't cotton to strangers much. Prob'ly under the bed, if they're not outside huntin' theirselves a snack. Say, that reminds me. I shot a couple of rabbits last night and made me some stew. You want some? It's right good. I'm an okay cook, doin' for myself all these years."

I was suddenly, unwillingly, touched with sympathy. There was something in that last remark, a wistfulness, a shy pride—but I still wasn't prepared to risk ptomaine. "I'll bet it's delicious, but Alan and I are still not quite up to eating much. Jet lag?"

Surely even he had heard of jet lag. He did have a television, after all.

"Man, I know all about that. When I come back from 'Nam, I wasn't up to nothin' for a week. Long ways back, that was, but I still recollect how sick I was. 'Course, I hadn't had no good food for a long time in that cage they put me in." He finished his beer, belched, and crumpled the can in one huge fist. "Okay. So you want to hear about the professor. What you want to know?"

"Anything you can tell us, Jerry. You said he didn't have many visitors. That surprises me a little. He had so many friends."

"Yeah, but you know how it is. People get busy, they move away, they figger somebody else is goin' to keep the old man company. They got their own lives. Just like you."

The guilt that I had tried to lull to sleep stirred and stretched itself. Alan's hand closed over mine, and he took up the conversation.

"I trust, at least, that someone looked in on him regularly. At his age, almost anything could have happened.''

''Oh, they was a few people now and then. But as for reg'lar, that was me. I'd go see him every day. He didn't get out much anymore, only to the store for food and that. So mostly I'd find him in that workshop of his.''

''Workshop?'' I frowned.

''Yeah, the glass. You know.''

''No. What was he doing with glass?''

''Gee, maybe he took that up after you left. How long ago'd you say that was?''

''Over three years ago, now.''

''Yeah, I guess maybe it was after that. He was gettin' restless, see. He didn't go to work in the lab no more, said he couldn't see good enough.''

''Yes, he'd given that up even before Frank died. It was hard on him, but he was very firm about it. He said he wasn't going to be one of those old bores who got in the way of the young people and messed up their experiments. As if he would!''

''Yeah, well, when he quit, it left him with nothin' much to do with his time. And I guess he went to one of them art fairs, up in Brown County or somewheres, and he got interested in that stuff they do with colored glass. So he built hisself a workshop out back and took it up.''

''He started working in stained glass? At—what— ninety-three, ninety-four?''

''Yep. Pretty good at it, too. People come and give him stuff to do for them, whaddaya call it—''

''Commissions?''

''Yeah, that's it. He was real proud of that. Did right pretty stuff. Give me one last Christmas.'' He gestured toward a dirty window where a sun-catcher hung crook-edly from a rusty wire.

I had missed it when I first came in, overlooked it in the general clutter. Now I couldn't take my eyes off it. A swirl of abstract color, it glowed like a costly jewel in a pinchbeck setting.

"Don't know what it's supposed to be, but I kinda like it," said Jerry.

My throat was too tight to answer. Once more Alan stepped into the breach.

"It's a beautiful thing, Jerry. Do you remember who came to give Professor Cassidy commissions? We'd like to see more of his work."

"Lots of it in the workshop. I could take you over and see it."

"That would be very kind of you, and we'd like to do that. But we—my wife—would also like to talk to the people who saw the professor close to his death, if you remember who any of them are."

I marveled at Alan's patience. I was longing to get out of the smelly trailer, see Kevin's workshop, learn something—anything—that might be of use. My hus-band the policeman was able to set aside impatience, prod gently, get anything Jerry might be able to give us.

It worked, too, at last. "Sure I remember! Didn't I tell you I seen everything went on over there? Lemme see, now. The last week or two before he went to the hospital, you mean?"

"Or even before that."

"Don't know how far back I can recollect. But them last few days, sure, 'cause seemed like they was a lot of 'em."

I held my breath while Jerry searched his trauma-addled brain.

"They was the doctor, for one. Not his real doctor, but another one. I reckon he sent for him, on account of his real doctor was out of town. Got no business goin' away, doctors, if you ask me."

"You mean a doctor actually came to see him?" I spoke up. "A house call?"

Alan looked puzzled and opened his mouth, but now was not the time to explain that American doctors, unlike their English counterparts, stopped making house calls years ago. I frowned at my husband, and he closed his mouth again.

"Yeah, I thought it was kind of funny, too, but I guess, the prof bein' so old and all—"

"Probably. That was just before he went to the hospital, then?"

"Yeah. And before that—well, they was the lady lives next door. She wanted him to make her some glass, I reckon, 'cause she went out to the workshop. You might go to her house, if you want, but you won't see nothin', 'cause he never had time to finish whatever he was doin' for her. Then they was the cop."

I swear our ears pricked up like a cat's.

"A policeman? What was he doing there?"

"Not just *a* cop, *the* cop. Chief of po-lice." The accent was on the first syllable, and the tone was one of infinite contempt. I was extremely glad I hadn't mentioned Alan's profession.

"Come there for the same thing as everybody else, I reckon—wanted the prof to make him some glass. Don't know what no cop wants with somethin' nice like that."

I didn't speculate, but willed Jerry to continue.

He scratched his head. "Oh, then they was the preacher. He come round 'bout once a month, tryin' to sell the prof religion."

"What preacher was that? A priest, was it? Kevin was a good Catholic."

"Naah. Wasn't no priest, didn't wear no round collar or nothin'. Just the preacher from down the road. He was always preachin' hellfire and damnation and sayin' Catholics was idol-worshipers and that. I could hear him, summers when the windows was open, all the way over here. The prof never paid him no never mind, but he never throw him out, neither. He'd just listen, polite-like, and after a while the preacher'd run down and leave." Jerry guffawed, an alarming noise. "The prof told me onc't, he said he just turned off his hearin' aid till the preacher give up."

Alan chuckled. "That's one way to deal with a pest. When my hearing gets a little worse, I'll have to remember that. Jerry, did none of his family come to call?"

"He don't—didn't have much family in these parts. Just a niece or somethin'. Yeah, she come once or twice. Come for a handout, I reckon. Way I hear it, her husband's just run off with some broad, and she don't got much money.

"And that's about it, near as I can recollect, 'cept for the lady lawyer. She come once. Kept a close eye on her, you can bet. Don't reckon a woman got no business bein' a lawyer. Didn't trust her. 'Sides—she ain't bad to look at in them short skirts she wears, y'know?"

He gave Alan a sly look; Alan winked. Well, really! I'd deal with him later!

Alan continued his gentle probing for a few minutes more, but Jerry had evidently given us all the information he could remember. When he repeated, for the third time, his invitation to share rabbit stew, we decided it was time to leave.

"Don't you want to see the workshop?" He sounded just a little forlorn.

"We do, very much, but I have an appointment in a few minutes. Can we come back another time?"

"Any time you want. I'm always here, almost. Next time come for supper."

"We'll take you up on that, Jerry," promised my husband, to my dismay. "It's been a pleasure to meet you."

"Same here. You want to know anything about the prof, you just come and ask me!"

SIX

"DO YOU REALLY propose to eat something he's cooked?" I demanded when we were out of earshot. "And what about that wink and leer you two exchanged?"

"Cementing diplomatic relations, my dear," said Alan blandly. "Not to mention the fact that it isn't wise to offend murder suspects."

"Murder suspect? Jerry? He's a little strange, I know, but he was obviously devoted to Kevin."

"He was also a prisoner of war in Vietnam—did you catch that?"

"Of course," I said loftily.

"Of course. Well, that was an experience that left a good many men with some peculiar ideas. *And* he's a crack shot with that rifle of his."

"How do you know that?"

"He shot two rabbits last night. One rabbit isn't too hard to bag, but the first shot scares any others around. They'll freeze for a second or two and then hare off, if you'll excuse the expression. He'd have to reload the gun, sight, and hit a small running target. That takes skill."

It's amazing, the things I don't know. "Okay. Point taken. But Kevin wasn't shot, and I think Jerry was Kevin's faithful dog."

"Dogs can turn vicious. I'm keeping an open mind, and I'm keeping relations with Jerry very, very friendly. Now, do you want to call on that neighbor, investigate Kevin's house, or get some lunch?"

"Hah! You, my dear, are the most excellent and civilized of men, and you know all about hunting rabbits. But even you don't know everything. Any woman knows you don't go knocking on somebody's door at lunchtime. And we can't get near Kevin's house while Jerry's on guard. We eat lunch."

"Right. What sort of food did you have in mind?"

"Anything but rabbit."

I'd intended a quick salad at my favorite little café on the edge of town. Scratch that idea. The café was now a used bookstore next to a mini-mall I'd never seen before. I drove around the outskirts of town, getting more frustrated by the moment. The streets kept turning out wrong. Almost all the old landmarks were gone; in their place were housing developments and condominiums and chain stores and fast-food joints.

"Three years, Alan! Only three years! How could it change so much in that time?"

"I imagine it's the outlying areas. The city center and the residential areas probably haven't changed much."

I shut up. I was absolutely not ready even to talk about the residential areas. I might, before we left Hillsburg, get up the courage to drive past my old house, but not yet. Not yet. If they'd torn that down, or cut down my beloved trees, or—no.

Failing to find any reasonable place to eat, in the end we settled for a fast-food hamburger and climbed back into the car feeling full, greasy, and unsatisfied. And I, for one, was in no sweet temper.

"For two cents I'd go back to the hotel and pull the covers over my head."

The only response to a remark like that is to ignore it. Alan said, "The neighbor first, do you think? Or one of the others?"

I turned the key in the ignition. "We might as well try her. It's Saturday. With any luck she'll be home. Most of the others we can beard in their offices next week, but we don't know where she works. Or *if* she works outside the home."

"Right. And by that reasoning, tomorrow we'll take on the preacher. Yes?"

I sighed and made a risky left turn out of the parking lot. "I was," I said when we were safely in the traffic lanes again, "looking forward to my old church tomorrow. But I suppose duty calls."

We were approaching Kevin's neighborhood by a different route than the one I had taken earlier, and when we got near, I stopped the car in utter dismay. The neat little farmhouses that used to dot the road were gone. In their place were a huge plot of bulldozed earth and a sign indicating that a new superstore was to be built on the site.

"Look at that! People uprooted! The countryside ruined! How can they *do* that?"

Alan quieted my fulminations, and I turned in the direction of the only house now close enough to Kevin's to be considered "next door." A country "next door," for sure: about a quarter of a mile along a narrow back road.

"This'll be gone soon, too, I suppose!"

"Perhaps not. It's a pleasant house, certainly."

I like to think I can tell something about people by the houses they live in. This one was an old farmhouse, white and rambling. The front porch sagged a bit, but it, like the rest of the house, was bright with fresh paint. A big pot of red geraniums blazed in a patch of sunlight by the front steps.

The woman who answered the door did fit the house. She was dressed in blue jeans that were clean and well fitting, but not chic. Her white shirt probably belonged to her husband, and her short gray hair was in wild disarray. Her face, shiny with soap, didn't need makeup. She was quite beautiful.

"Yes? If you're with Jehovah's Witnesses or the Mormons, I'm sorry, but I'm very busy."

I wished I dared laugh at the expression on my husband's face. "No," I said hastily. "We're not trying to convert you or sell you anything. I apologize for not calling ahead, but we didn't know your name."

The woman looked puzzled. She also looked ready to close the door.

"All we knew," I said quickly, "was that you were a neighbor of Kevin Cassidy's. I don't think we've ever met, but I was a good friend of Kevin's in years past, and if you have a moment or two, I'd really like to talk to you about him."

"Oh. Sure, come on in. I'm sort of in the middle of something, but I'd be glad to talk about Kevin. A real shame about him, wasn't it?"

She showed us into a small living room that looked just like her. It was clean and reasonably tidy except for piles of papers tumbled over the coffee table. It was comfortable, but not fashionable. The quilted cushions scattered here and there looked as if love had gone into them; the pictures were mostly family photographs. I felt immediately at home.

We introduced ourselves and sat down. Her name was Hannah Schneider.

"That's one of Kevin's pieces, isn't it?" I gestured to a small window by the fireplace. Its original glass had been replaced by a glowing piece of art, abstract but charged with life.

"Yes, isn't it gorgeous? We were all just blown away when he suddenly revealed all that talent. He was a genius in glass, really."

"A genius, period. I knew him mostly as a scientist—and a friend, of course."

"He was a good friend to me," said Hannah with a sad smile. "He even—well, I was one of his students, of course. I think—were you related to Frank Martin?"

"He was my first husband. He died several years ago."

"Oh yes, I'd heard. I was his student, too, for a year of botany. And then when I went on to pharmacy school, I gave those two men most of the credit for my grades. They gave me such a thorough grounding in scientific method, I got through pharmacy school with no sweat."

"You're a pharmacist, then?"

"Part-time. I didn't work at all while I was raising my kids, but now that they're grown up and on their own, it helps pass the time. I may give it up again, though. I've gotten involved in community work." She gestured to the card table full of papers.

"Is that what you were in the middle of? It looks like a lot of work."

"Massive, but worth it—if we can only win!"

Hannah sat forward on her chair, her eyes alight. She began to talk eagerly, her hands making rapid gestures and now and then running through her hair, making it stand straight up.

"You've seen the abomination they've foisted on us across the road? The new superstore? Well, some of us are fed up. We've had enough. They sneaked the superstore past us, but there's this shopping mall they're trying to put up out south of town, and we're fighting it tooth and nail."

"Good for you! I've been getting more and more upset about how much Hillsburg has changed, just in the few years I've been gone."

Hannah nodded vigorously. "Fine old buildings torn down, for no reason at all! Good farmland turned into a parking lot! It's a crime, that's what it is. Every town looking exactly alike—well, we don't need it here in Hillsburg. Kevin agreed, incidentally—even contributed to the cause. And we've got a good shot at stopping them, too...."

She expounded on her theme for some time, but with Alan and me as audience, she was preaching to the choir. When she finally slowed down and I could get a word in edgewise, I said, "Well, I agree with every word you say, and I wish you all the luck. But you said you had only a little time, and I had some things to ask you—"

"Oh, Lord, I got on my soapbox, didn't I? Sorry. And I really do have to get busy. The meeting about the mall is tonight, here, and I've got lots of paperwork to deal with beforehand. So how can I help you?"

"I'm just trying to get a picture of Kevin's last few weeks. He was a good friend, and I feel awful that I lost touch with him and let him die without a chance to say good-bye."

Hannah sobered. "I know how you feel. It came as a shock to me, too. We all thought he was healthy as a horse. I hadn't seen much of him myself—too busy organizing the antimall forces. And then all of a sudden, there he was in the hospital."

"But—I must be confused. Somebody told me he thought you'd been over to Kevin's workshop just a few days before he got sick. Ordering a new window, I thought he said?"

"Oh, good grief, you're right and I'm wrong. I did talk to him about the possibility of doing one for a friend. We didn't settle anything definite, though. I'd forgotten all about it. Who on earth told you? I didn't think I'd mentioned it to anyone."

"I'm not sure. One of the other neighbors, I think."

"There aren't any other neighbors, really, except that crazy man in the trailer." Her voice sharpened. "I'd be careful about him, if I were you. He's a menace, and that pigsty he lives in! A disgrace to the countryside, that's what he is! I wouldn't believe too much he tells you." She shook her head and glanced at her watch. I had to take the hint.

"Yes, we really must go. Do you mind if I come back sometime and just talk about Kevin? I'd call first, of course."

"Any time, but do call." She had recovered her gracious manner. "I'm going to be out a lot, drumming up support for the cause and talking to lawyers, and all. Nice to meet both of you."

We were shooed out the door, quite nicely but very efficiently. I backed out of the driveway and drove out of sight before stopping. I stretched back, my arms stiff against the steering wheel.

"Well, now what? That sure didn't get us anywhere."

"A lady with a mission," said Alan a little dryly. "Missionaries are often somewhat—monotonous, shall we say?"

"I liked her."

"My dear, so did I, though she got a little shrill on the subject of Jerry, didn't she? I simply wished she would moderate her enthusiasm a trifle, even though I agree with her point of view.

"Now," he added briskly, "shall we go on to the next person on the list? I'm beginning to get very interested in this wild-goose chase of yours, Dorothy."

SEVEN

THE NEXT PERSON on the list, we decided after a quick conference, was either the attending doctor in Kevin's last illness or the police chief, whichever could be found easily on a Saturday afternoon.

"Let's try the police chief first," I suggested. "At least we know where to look for him. And if he isn't working today, we can try the doctor."

So we drove back into town, where the police station, thank heaven, was still where it had always been.

Yes, the chief was in. Yes, we could see him. Names, please?

Here, at least, was a place where Alan's title might be useful. "Dorothy Martin. And Chief Constable Alan Nesbitt, from the county of Belleshire, England."

"You don't say. Official business?"

"No," said Alan firmly. "Merely a courtesy call."

The desk sergeant scratched his head and spoke into the telephone. I frowned at Alan.

"My dear, I cannot operate under false pretenses," he said quietly. "And I am, I remind you, not the chief constable anymore."

"It never hurts to throw your weight around a little," I whispered back.

Which just goes to show how wrong I can be.

We were given visitors' badges. I was a little surprised

at that formality, but Hillsburg tries to keep its civic departments up-to-date. When we were shown back to the office occupied by the chief, though, it seemed very small-town. It was a shabby, homey place—imitation knotty pine paneling, scarred wooden desk covered with pictures of the chief's family. I glanced at them, looked more closely, and then looked at the chief's name badge with dawning recognition.

"Lacey! Darryl Lacey! My word, I wouldn't have known you, but your son looks exactly the way you did in fourth grade."

He grinned. "He does, doesn't he? Now me, I've put on a little weight. And lost a little hair. But I was sure you'd figure out who I was, Mrs. Martin. What're you doing back in town?"

He was bald as an egg, indeed resembled an egg: He could have played Humpty Dumpty in any production of *Alice in Wonderland*.

"Oh, we've been meaning to come for a visit for some time," I prevaricated. "Darryl, this is my husband, Alan Nesbitt. Alan, Darryl was one of my students, oh, years ago, now."

I beamed at both of them. Alan extended his hand. Darryl took it and said stiffly, "How do you do, sir."

Uh-oh.

"Won't you sit down?"

He was being very formal now. Alan tried to set him at ease. "Mr. Lacey, I hope you don't mind our dropping in on you like this. I'm sure you're very busy."

"Not as busy as all that. We don't go in for all the spit and polish that you guys do in your country. Just a rough and ready small-town police force, that's all we have here. Drunk and disorderly, auto theft, domestic violence, a bank robbery now and then. We manage."

"Er—the students give you no trouble, then?"

"That's what the campus police are for. We deal with 'em when they get into trouble off campus. Which they usually don't. And if it's drugs you're thinking of, we don't have too much problem with that here, not yet, no matter what you've heard about Americans."

Worse and worse. I stepped in. "Darryl—oh, dear, I suppose I should call you Chief Lacey, but—"

"You call me anything you want, Mrs. Martin." There was just the faintest emphasis on the *you*. He had turned away from Alan and addressed only me.

"Darryl, then, since I knew you when you were a pup. We really don't want to take up your time, but I wondered what you could tell me about the last few weeks of Kevin Cassidy's life. I understand you were a friend of his. I was so sorry to hear of his death." I repeated my story of concern and guilt feelings, a story that, however true, was beginning to sound very thin to me. I hoped Darryl found it more convincing.

"Yeah, he was a great old guy—a real character. He even gave me some money once. You know about those 'loans' of his?"

"Yes, Frank and I borrowed some once, ourselves. He was a generous man, Kevin."

"I guess there's not hardly anybody in town didn't borrow a little from the prof at one time or another. I was taking a course from him, back when I was a freshman, and I wanted to buy a car so bad I could taste it. He advanced me the money. Gave me a lecture along with it, about being careful, not drinking and driving, all that. I don't s'pose I'd have listened to it coming from anybody else, but he had a way of sounding like God, you know?"

"I do indeed. I didn't know you went to the university, Darryl."

"Dropped out after a couple of years and went into the police. I've never been sorry. College wasn't for me, but I enjoyed some of it. 'Specially the prof's course. I don't know what a world-famous guy like him was doing teaching freshman biology, but he sure made it interesting."

"He insisted on teaching that course now and then. Used to say he liked to keep in touch with the real world, the people who didn't think biology was the be-all and end-all of life. So did you see much of him the last few years?"

"Not a lot. I used to drop in once in a while. Kind of worried about him living out there all by himself, you know? He wasn't getting any younger. And I went out once, just before he got sick, to see if he could make me one of those glass things he'd started doing. Present for my wife. You know about the glass stuff?"

"I've seen a few examples of his work. He was a real artist."

"Yeah, who'd have thought a guy could take up something new, at his age, and be so good at it?"

"He was a remarkable man. How did he seem when you saw him?"

"Fine. We had a cold spell in August, and I went out mostly to make sure he was keeping warm enough, but it was almost hot out there in that workshop of his, what with the soldering iron and all, and he was working away, happy as a clam. Didn't seem sick at all. You could have knocked me over with a feather when I heard he had pneumonia."

"A soldering iron?"

"You put the glass together with solder. I don't know

how it works, exactly, but there was a big reel of the stuff on his workbench. Along with copper foil and lots of different colors of glass—gosh, it was pretty. I feel real bad he never got a chance to finish mine. And who told you I was a friend of his?''

The question came so suddenly I had no answer ready. ''Umm—one of the neighbors, I think—''

''He didn't have any close neighbors, nobody to see who was coming and going. Except that crazy guy in the woods. It was him, wasn't it?''

''Really, I—''

''Never mind. I suppose you don't want me to know what he said about me. He doesn't like the police much, and the feeling's mutual. One of these days he's going to go too far with that squirrel rifle of his and kill somebody. He's a menace.''

I should have kept my mouth shut, but I couldn't help protesting. ''Oh, Darryl, he's harmless enough, surely? A little eccentric, not terribly bright, but—''

''Eccentric! He's crazy as a coot! He tell you about Vietnam?''

''A little.''

''He tell you he was in the psych ward for a couple of years after he got back?''

I didn't answer.

''No, I didn't think so. Look, I feel kind of sorry for the guy, myself, but he's more'n a few plays short of a football game. The gooks really messed up his head when he was a POW, see. He tried to kill a guard when he was in the loony bin, and he can't be trusted. He just goes haywire sometimes, and he's way too good a shot to be safe. I've seen him shoot a running mouse from twenty, thirty feet away. I wouldn't go out there anymore if I were you, Mrs. Martin.''

I opened my mouth to ask another question about Kevin, but the radio on Darryl's shoulder went into action. I couldn't hear what the crackling voice said, but Darryl got up in a hurry. "Sorry, Mrs. Martin, but I gotta go. Nice to see you again." Without so much as a nod to Alan he sped out the door, leaving us to find our own way out of the station.

We drove back to the hotel in silence, but when we got to the room I had to deal with it.

"Alan, I'm so sorry. I should have realized—"

"Never mind, love. It's only natural that your old friends should resent me. It's all right."

"But Darryl isn't an old friend. He's just a child I taught. And still acting pretty childish, if you ask me."

"He was afraid I was going to lord it over him, as the senior officer in an English police force. It was his inferiority complex at work. I'm afraid we've developed a worldwide reputation as snobs about our policing methods. And quite justified, too."

"Your reputation, or your snobbery?"

"Both, actually."

I giggled at that, but I wasn't quite ready to let it go. "I don't know what you must think of the hick town I lived in all my life."

"Now who's developing an inferiority complex? Come on, let's sit down and work out what we've got, if anything."

I dug the notebook out from under the stack of sweatshirts, but there was discouragingly little to put in it. Under the heading "Who was present?" I added the names Jerry had given us, or the descriptions where we didn't know names. And we were able to add a little information to the "Interviews" section.

"Okay. Police chief. Doesn't like you."

"Irrelevant," Alan objected.

"Maybe. Maybe not. It stays. Called on Kevin shortly before he died."

"Borrowed money from him," Alan contributed.

"Are you still harping on that money? I don't see how it could have anything to do with anything."

"If his attitude toward me stays in, the money stays in."

I sighed and made the note. "And he took one course from Kevin. Relevant?"

"Probably not, but write it down. At this stage we have no idea what is important and what isn't."

"I suspect nobody; I suspect everybody," I chanted in an Inspector Clouseau voice.

"Exactly. On to Mrs. Schneider."

There wasn't much to say about her, either. A pharmacist by profession, a former student of Kevin's, a fanatic about keeping development out of Hillsburg.

"I wonder," asked Alan, "how much money the professor gave her for this project of hers."

"She didn't say."

"No. But she must need quite a lot. Attorneys who can take on mall developers with any chance of winning don't come cheap."

"I don't see why you think it's important, but we could ask her, I suppose."

"If there's no other way to find out. Would there be public records?"

"If the protest group has officially registered as a not-for-profit organization, I suppose there might be. Though if Kevin gave her the money and she then plowed it into the protest fund, it would probably just be listed as her contribution."

"It's worth looking into, on Monday when the records office opens. Where would it be in an American city?"

"County courthouse, I imagine. I really don't know a thing about it, but that'd be the place to start looking. And this is the county seat, so it'll be easy, if boring."

"Police work," said Alan didactically, "is often boring. Almost all of the time, in fact. The other fraction of the time it's entirely too exciting. When, for example, one deals with unbalanced people carrying rifles."

Sighing again, I added Jerry's name to my list. If there was too little to say about either Darryl or Mrs. Schneider, there was too much about Jerry.

"Rifleman; excellent shot," I wrote. "Alan, I still insist that has nothing to do with anything. Kevin wasn't shot."

"Why are you so partial to our gun-toting friend? Who, I might add, has attitudes toward women that usually infuriate you."

"I don't know, exactly. Yes, he's a male chauvinist, and he's not very clean or very bright. Not the sort I'd usually want for a friend. But I feel sorry for him. And he likes cats."

"Neither of which consideration disqualifies him as a suspect."

"No. What else should I write down?"

"Belligerent. Nearest neighbor. Received gifts from Professor Cassidy. Perhaps money? Probably mentally disturbed. Large and apparently strong. Dislikes authority figures."

I dutifully recorded it all. "All right, all right. But if you get all that, I get this." And added: "Devoted to Kevin; his faithful protector."

Alan read the whole account over and shook his head.

"It's little enough for a day's work. Should we try to seek out one of the other possibilities?"

"Not if I get a vote. We're too muddled. We need to let the thing sit for a while. Anyway, the stores will still be open for another couple of hours, and I want to hit that mystery bookstore!"

Alan grinned, ostentatiously checked his wallet, and followed me out the door.

The London mystery bookshops don't always carry a great selection of American authors, and when they do, the books cost a lot more than they would in America. I was way behind on Barbara D'Amato and Carolyn Hart and Jane Langton and Carole Nelson Douglas and a score of others. By the time we left the store I had enough reading material to last me for weeks.

"It'll cost a young fortune to ship those back to England," Alan complained.

"Not to mention several pounds of tigers in various forms."

He said no more.

Right after dinner I started on a book by an author new to me. It was set in a nursing home and concerned skulduggery among the staff, who were, sometimes with the help of moneygrubbing relatives, defrauding the elderly residents left and right. Despite the fact that it kept me awake until the wee hours, I woke bright and early Sunday morning with a brand-new idea.

"Alan, we have to see Ms. Carmichael in the morning. First thing."

"Very well. If we can get an appointment, of course. Am I allowed to ask why?"

"Not yet," I said smugly. "I have an idea, that's all. I want to see if it pans out before I tell you about it."

EIGHT

WE WENT TO two church services that Sunday, an excessive number in my opinion. We were up early enough to hit the first service at St. Paul's, the lovely old Episcopal church where I'd been baptized and confirmed and married, the conservative Anglo-Catholic church I'd loved all my life.

I came out in a state of shock.

"Alan, a woman priest! And Rite II! The old liturgy was beautiful, and reverent, and dignified. This new one—" Words failed me.

"Hardly new, surely. The revisers have been at it for years, love—in England, too, you know."

"I know, but the old priest at St. Paul's kept things the way they were. I'll bet this—this person they've got now can't even remember the 1928 prayer book!"

"The important things are still the same," said Alan firmly.

"Sez you! And I put on one of my favorite hats, too," I added with utter irrelevance.

After the second service we attended, however, I was forced humbly to admit that my husband could be right. If St. Paul's had abandoned many of the outward and visible signs that were dear to me, the inward and spiritual grace was, for the most part, still there. It was conspicuously missing from Parson Bussey's church.

The building, though rather small and shabby, was a standard white frame church with a dispirited steeple and narrow gothic windows. Plain, somewhat dirty windows looked out on a cornfield on one side and an old cemetery on the other, with a rather run-down house, presumably the parsonage, next to the cemetery.

The preacher himself was a tall, gaunt man with the dark, sunken eyes of the fanatic. From the first it was obvious that loving kindness was not the order of the day at the Church of the All-Consuming Fire.

"At least there aren't any snakes," I said in an undertone, halfway through the lengthy, ranting sermon.

"Yet," Alan replied ominously.

There were no snakes, but everything else that could be dreamed up by a somewhat demented fundamentalist mind was incorporated into the morning's exercises. I refused, even in my mind, to call it a worship service. The all-pervading theme was the hell-horror that awaited the sinner. The way to avoid the flames and pitchforks, apparently, was to purge from one's life anything resembling joy, to exhort one's friends and neighbors to do the same, and to devote one's worldly goods to the church in order to speed its message.

"Alan, we shouldn't have come. I don't think I can stand any more." They were singing a loud hymn in which the torments of hell were described in excruciating detail and equally excruciating rhyme.

"We can't leave now. Surely it'll be over soon. Then we can have a word with the—er—leader, and slip away."

It wasn't that easy. I'd thought the hymn was the last gasp, but everyone sat down again after the Amen, and Parson Bussey went back to the pulpit to make announcements. The sermon that evening was to be entitled "The Devil within Us." Everyone was instructed to attend and bring a neighbor. The Thursday-night prayer meeting would be at the home of Brother Graber, immediately after supper. Attendance had been dropping off, the parson said menacingly, and added grim warnings to the effect that if the congregation was really interested in salvation, they'd better forget about television Thursday night and show up to spend an evening wrestling in prayer. Television, it appeared, was the devil's own invention anyway.

There was a little stirring among the flock at that pronouncement. I sensed dissension in the ranks, especially among the men who wanted to watch Thursday-night football, but nobody's remarks were clearly audible. This congregation might not always agree with their preacher, but they were afraid of him.

Or else they hold him in awe, I told myself. Don't let your own prejudices influence your ideas, Dorothy.

Everyone was to remember, Parson Bussey went on, that next Saturday was the day appointed for painting the church. He expected all able-bodied men to help, and announced that the ladies would prepare a luncheon for the workers. Something about the expression on the female faces in the congregation told me that was the first they'd heard of it, but again, no one protested.

There was a brief pause. Was he finished at last?

No.

"Brethren, we have this morning two visitors among us. Praise the Lord that two sinners have seen the light and been moved to join us! Brother and Sister, will you come up and tell us your names, that we may pray for your salvation from the terrible toils of sin and damnation?"

There may be worse fates than being hauled up with

one's dignified English husband before a fire-breathing preacher and then being prayed over, at length. Yes, just possibly there may be, but I wouldn't like to say for sure. I, myself, have been in danger of my life more than once, and I don't recall those experiences as being anything like as horrific as this one. *My* only prayer during the ordeal, that a thunderbolt would come down from heaven and strike us all instantly dead, was not answered. The sky remained blue and serene, and the preacher's instructions to God continued.

After an eternity or two, it was finally over. The last of the curious flock dispersed, and we were left alone with Parson Bussey, who had seized Alan's arm and was apparently prepared to preach at him indefinitely. I wanted, urgently, to go home and take a lengthy shower, but one look at Alan's face told me I'd have to wait awhile. He'd suffered, and he didn't intend that his suffering should be in vain.

The preacher finally gave him an opening. "Brother Nesbitt, what holy inspiration led you and your good wife to seek out salvation this morning? To leave the paths of idol worship and the ways of the devil and repent? To tread the narrow way of salvation and leave behind the fleshpots—"

"Actually," said Alan in crisp English accents, "it was more a matter of wanting to talk to you."

Parson Bussey looked severely annoyed at being cut off in the middle of his peroration. "Brother, it is I who should talk to you, to save you—"

"We wanted a word or two about Professor Cassidy."

The preacher dropped his viselike grip of Alan's arm. "You knew the professor?"

"No. My wife, however, had been his friend for many years."

Parson Bussey, like Jerry, apparently preferred to ignore my existence, but he turned to me now with a frown. "Sister Nesbitt—"

I'd had enough. "My name is Martin. *Mrs.* Martin."

"But—this man *is* your husband?"

"Yes."

Oh, you're one of those, said his look. "*Sister* Martin, I'm sorry to hear you associated with Mr. Cassidy. He was a grave sinner, an idolator, who refused to listen to the word of the Lord. I tremble for him now, suffering the torments of the damned—"

"Mr. Bussey." I had the pleasure of his reaction to the title. He got everybody else's wrong, but he didn't like it when I refused to give him any honorary address. His mouth set in a hard line. "Mr. Bussey, Dr. Cassidy was my friend for many years. He was one of the finest men I've ever known, and a devout Catholic. I'm quite sure you don't need to worry about his eternal fate. And it wasn't my impression that he refused to hear your—your message. I was told you visited him shortly before his death."

"And where did you get that information?" His face was so granitelike I was surprised he could move his lips.

"I don't remember. It doesn't matter. I simply wanted to talk to anybody who talked to him in those last few weeks, see how he was feeling, if he was happy. If you didn't see him, fine." I wanted that shower more than ever.

"I didn't say I didn't see him. It was my duty to spread the word of the Lord to him, however much he might insult me. The last time I called on him was about a week before he was taken sick. We talked for almost an hour. I am sorry to say it was a complete waste of my time. He remained as stubborn as ever. I wondered at times if he was even listening!"

I remembered about the hearing aid and felt a little better. Kevin had managed to put one over on the preacher.

"However, you will be happy to know that he did do one thing that may yet save him from some of the agonies of hellfire. Perhaps I moved his heart after all. Perhaps he knew that his soul was soon to be required of him. That last time I saw him he lent me some money, interest-free, for the use of my church. It enabled us to buy the paint we need so badly, and will facilitate other repairs. I trust"—he turned back to Alan—"that you will wish to help with the painting. It is a holy work, making seemly the house of God."

"So sorry," Alan murmured. "I believe we're expected at the synagogue that day, aren't we, Dorothy?" He nodded briefly to the preacher, whose mouth had dropped open, and led me away without another word.

"Synagogue, indeed," I said to him in the car. "That was wicked of you. I just wish I'd thought of it."

"Well, my dear, I had to do something, and kicking the man in the teeth seemed neither wise nor charitable." He glanced in the side mirror. "Do start the car, love. I believe he has thought of something else he wants to say to us."

I gunned the engine and shot off with a squeal that many a teenage boy would have admired. "If I ever see that man again," I said fervently, "it'll be way too soon. That was the worst couple of hours I've ever spent in my life."

"A policeman's lot—or even an amateur sleuth's—is not a happy one," Alan agreed. "It's a good thing the effort wasn't totally wasted. We learned one thing."

"The money. You know, Alan, I'm beginning to think you have a point about the money. And I don't intend to say one word more about it until tomorrow."

"The lawyer?"

"The lawyer. And, come to think of it, we did get one other little bit of information out of that disgusting performance."

"If you are referring to any fragment of theological wisdom—"

"Don't be silly. No, it's just that we've met the first person who didn't like Kevin. That could be significant, don't you think? And now that's enough of that. I don't want to talk about it anymore. I've got to get to a shower and wash off the smell of curdled piety."

We spent a pleasant afternoon, walking over the campus, searching out tigers. I got enough exercise to be more than ready for an early night. Just as I was falling asleep, Alan murmured one last comment.

"Hmmm?"

"I was remembering what you said about the people in your hometown. How friendly they were."

I was too sleepy even to retaliate.

MONDAY MORNING I got lucky. An early call to Ms. Carmichael's office reached only the receptionist, but she said that a scheduled court date had been postponed, and Ms. Carmichael was therefore free all morning. If we could come in about ten?

"Ten it is," I said jubilantly, and hung up.

"I heard that," said Alan, coming out of the bathroom clad in a towel. "We've time for a leisurely breakfast, then."

"Plenty of time, especially—listen, my dearest love,

I don't want you to take this the wrong way, but I don't want you to come with me this morning."

His expressive eyebrows rose. "The secret sleuth at work?"

"Don't be silly. No, it's just that she has a down on men right now. The lawyer, I mean. She's divorced, and quite recently, is my guess."

"You're right about that."

"How do you know? I was just going by the level of bitterness in her voice when she talked about it."

"Ah, women and their intuition." I threw a pillow at him. "As a mere male, I rely on evidence. There was still a pale stripe on her ring finger. She's removed her wedding ring only recently."

I looked at him admiringly. The towel had slipped when he dodged the pillow, so it was not only his mind I was admiring. Alan in his late sixties is still a fine figure of a man.

"GOOD MORNING, Mrs. Martin. I presume you brought me your expense account?"

Even for a lawyer, the woman was a model of brisk efficiency. I needed to slow things down a little, work for an us-girls-together atmosphere. "No, actually, it was something else I wanted to talk to you about, and I wish you'd call me Dorothy."

If I was hoping for a reciprocal invitation, I didn't get it. She simply nodded. "Dorothy it is, then. I'm at your disposal."

Well, I was ready, even if she was being more formal than I'd hoped. "You see, I've become worried about those expenses. They're fairly high, what with plane fare for two of us, and at the highest rates going, and then the hotel and all..." I waited for some response, but there was only an I'm-listening tilt to her head. I plunged ahead.

"You see, I've been talking to people about Kevin, his friends and neighbors, and it seems he was still making lots of his famous loans. You know about his loans?"

"Yes, indeed. I bought this practice from Dr. Cassidy's former attorneys, who drew up the paperwork for the loans." She hesitated and seemed about to say more, but finally shut her mouth firmly.

"Well, then, you know he laid out a lot of money over the years. And I know he never expected to be paid back, though I suppose some people did pay."

"Some."

A clam was loquacious by comparison. I struggled on. "Anyway, he's been retired for years, living on a pension and social security and whatever interest his investments brought in. And I'm just wondering. What with all the money he kept giving away, he surely couldn't have had a great deal left at the end. Will there really be enough in the estate to pay our expenses? Because if not, we're perfectly prepared—"

She tapped her pencil on the desk. "The estate has not yet been settled, of course," she said slowly.

"No, probate takes a long time. I know that. But surely you know how much will be left, roughly, after all his obligations are met. It's your job to know."

"Yes, I know." She tapped her pencil again, and then sighed. "Very well, Dorothy. I suppose it's a legitimate question. In any case, I will have to file a preliminary inventory of the estate fairly soon; the essentials will then be a matter of public record.

"I do not propose to give you any figures, but I will say that you are quite right in your suppositions. Dr.

Cassidy's charity had nearly exhausted his savings. I may say that both his bank officials and I tried to point out the dangers of his actions, but he refused to take us seriously.''

I nodded. ''I can just hear him. 'You can't take it with you' was always one of his favorite sayings.''

''However, you need not worry about your expenses. There is quite sufficient money left to meet them. Dr. Cassidy was very specific in saying that you and your husband were to stay in Hillsburg as long as you liked— no, I believe his exact phrase was 'as long as she thinks necessary'—at his expense.''

''I see.'' I was thinking fast. ''Ms. Carmichael, what would have happened when Kevin's money was completely gone? Would his pension and social security have been enough to keep him going? I'd hate to think of him living in poverty, after helping so many people all these years.''

''He spent very little on himself, you know, and his pension was reasonably generous. At his recent levels of expenditure, his resources would have been adequate.''

''Yet you and his bankers tried to talk him out of spending his savings. You spoke of 'dangers.' Why, if he was really going to have enough money?''

She rose, a wintry smile on her face. ''It is the nature of bankers and lawyers to wish to preserve money, Mrs. Martin. Now, if there's nothing else, I'm really very busy.''

She walked briskly out the door, leaving me staring after her, my mind working furiously.

She'd reverted to my surname. And why hadn't she answered my question?

NINE

"ANYTHING?" ALAN WAS lounging in the easy chair, his feet propped on another chair, when I came back to the hotel room. He tossed his book toward the bed; it slid off and landed upside down on the floor.

"I'm not sure. That is one very closemouthed lady." I reached down to retrieve the book, a thick, oversize paperback with a plain brown back cover. "What's this? It looks dull." I handed it back to him

"Not what one might call action-packed, but it has its points." He showed me the front.

"*Wills and Probate: The Basics of Settling an Estate,*" I read. "Good grief, Alan, are you a mind reader?"

"It was a fairly simple deduction, said Sherlock Holmes, tucking his violin under his chin and playing a few melancholy notes." Alan bowed his imaginary fiddle. "A man has died. You have gone to visit his solicitor. Ergo, you are interested in his estate. I thought I'd while away the time by consulting the law myself, so I searched in the bookshop next door and found this. It's written for the layman, so it's almost comprehensible. I was reasonably certain you wouldn't extract much information from Ms. Carmichael."

"You're right about that. She did, grudgingly, confirm

what I'd already guessed, that Kevin really didn't have much money left.''

"I'm curious about your working hypothesis. I'm certain you have one.''

"Well—it did enter my head that, if his great-niece was in serious need of money, she might have decided to speed Uncle Kevin on his way before he could give every cent of it to other people. That's assuming she was his principal heir. I'd hoped Carmichael the Clam might give me a few hints, but nothing doing.''

"Hmm. I'm not sure we have a credible motive there, Dorothy. If the woman needed money, could she not simply have asked the professor for it? He was spreading it about by the pailful, apparently.''

"*If* she was on good terms with him. He never talked about her, remember. Maybe there was some sort of family feud.''

"In that case, would he have been likely to leave his money to her?''

"Oh. I hadn't thought of that. It's so frustrating not to *know*.''

"Ah, that is precisely where my research will be of help. This book has a section that summarizes estate law for each of your fifty states. I looked up Indiana, and it appears quite likely that the professor's—sorry, Kevin's—estate will have been opened by now.''

"What does that mean?''

"It's the first step in probate. The details are somewhat technical, but the relevant point for our purposes is that the will is deposited with the court.''

"Which means?''

"Which means that it will be available for perusal upon application to the clerk of the court. Apparently for a small fee it can be copied.''

His bland smile reminded me more than ever of Alistair Cooke.

"For heaven's sake, why didn't you say so to begin with? What are we waiting for?"

We did, of course, have to wait. First we had to get to the courthouse. Not that there was any difficulty about that, but it required a bit of a walk. There was no point in trying to drive; I knew parking would be impossible. Hillsburg, the county seat, has a gigantic neo-Baroque courthouse sitting in a lovely green square, smack in the middle of town. All four streets approaching the square have to detour around it, an arrangement that stalls traffic, makes parking scarce, and creates near-gridlock on the days of home football games. The setup, in short, is absolutely typical of small-town midwestern courthouse squares.

I've always loved the magnificent ugliness of the old red sandstone building, its towers and abutments and niches and wings, but it's not what you would call a convenient sort of building. Once inside, one discovers that the floor plan is as labyrinthine as one would expect. Alan was fascinated with the place and insisted on peeking into the courtrooms and studying the statuary. It was half an hour before we found the office of the clerk of the circuit court in an obscure corner of the basement, and then she was, a sign on the locked door informed us, out to lunch. So we found ourselves a sandwich at a coffee shop and then wandered around the square to kill the rest of the time.

"That's the monument to the Civil War dead, Alan. And this fancy bronze one commemorates our soldiers lost in the two world wars. Far too many of them, both times."

Alan studied the plaques for a long time, and when

he turned back to me, his face was very sober. "One forgets, Dorothy. I wasn't around for the first war, of course, and I was only a boy in the forties. I knew there were Americans about, but I didn't quite take it in... .It was a great sacrifice for them to make, for a country and a people very far away from their homes."

"They were wars worth fighting, Alan. We weren't fighting for England, not really. We were fighting for a principle."

"Dangerous things, principles." He said it very seriously.

"Indeed. Lord Peter Wimsey once said much the same thing. 'The first thing a principle does is kill somebody' was more or less the way he put it."

The sun was warm, the trees in the square brilliantly beautiful. We found a bench and sat in thoughtful silence until it was time to go back inside the courthouse.

The clerk was back at work, and the minute I saw her, I recognized her.

"Good gracious, it's Becky Deming! Child, you haven't changed at all!"

"Mrs. Martin, of all people! Gosh, it's good to see you. I didn't know you were back in town. Have you moved back home?" She glanced at Alan.

"No, just visiting. Becky, this is my husband, Alan Nesbitt. Alan, this was one of my favorite students, though I tried not to let her know it. Becky Deming."

"It's Stevens now, Mrs. Martin. Do you remember Dick? He was a couple of classes ahead of me—"

"I certainly do! The bane of my existence that year. That boy could think up more mischief than any other six kids in that class. Has he straightened out?"

"Not much. He sometimes acts more like our boys' brother than their father." We both laughed. Becky's whole being radiated contentment. Dick had fulfilled his promise, then. He'd been not only the most active boy in his class but also the brightest, destined, I felt, for great things once he grew up a little. Here, at last, was someone who actually made me feel at home.

"So what brings you down here to the catacombs?"

"Pure curiosity, I have to admit. I was left a small bequest by dear old Dr. Cassidy—"

Becky's face clouded. "He was the nicest old man, wasn't he? I was really sorry when he died. Well, everybody was, I guess. He was the official Hillsburg character."

"A truly remarkable man. And I heard some rumors about how he left his money, and…well, it's none of my business, I know, but—"

"You want to see the will. Sure, no problem. If you want to have a seat, I'll find it for you. You want a copy?"

I started to say no, but Alan pressed my hand. "That would be very kind of you. We do have to be somewhere else shortly, and it would be convenient to take it with us."

Becky disappeared, and I raised my eyebrows at Alan. "In case it turns out we want to study it more carefully," he murmured, close to my ear. "It might raise suspicions if we glanced at it and *then* decided there was something that required further attention."

I shook my head. "Alan, every now and then I'm forced to admit there are good reasons why you rose to such exalted heights in your profession."

Becky exhibited no suspicion whatever about our motives. She came back in a few minutes with a photocopy of the will, accepted our dollar and a quarter copying fee, and waved good-bye. I couldn't wait to get back to the hotel and read Kevin's last wishes.

Five minutes after we sat down with it, I looked up at Alan, disappointment written all over my face.

"And another beautiful theory goes down in flames. Not a single bequest to anybody at all except me."

"And unless we suspect the entire biology department at Randolph University of conspiracy to murder, the residuary legatee is a washout, as well."

I sighed and flexed my aching shoulders. Our lack of progress was getting to me. "Are we just plain wrong, Alan? Was Kevin imagining things? Had he actually gotten senile while nobody was looking?"

"There was that accident on his steps, remember."

"It could have been just an accident."

"Yes."

"We forgot to ask Jerry about any others."

"Jerry, as an experience, is enough to make one forget everything except self-preservation. However, we hadn't that excuse with Mrs. Schneider."

"No. We got sidetracked, somehow. Anyway, Mrs. Schneider might not know. She isn't near enough to see his house, and I didn't get the idea she called on him very often. We could try Doc Foley."

"Wouldn't he have said, when his wife brought up the sprained ankle?"

"Maybe not. Doctors don't talk about their patients. But if we ask directly, I'll bet he'll tell us anything he knows."

So we got our car and set out for Dr. Foley's office, but it was a day for frustrations. The good doctor was at the hospital with a complicated obstetric case, and his secretary, new since my time, had no idea when he might be back. "Triplets," she said brightly. "I've rescheduled all his appointments. If it's urgent, you could see Dr. Boland. His office is just around the corner, and I don't think he's booked up this afternoon."

Dr. Boland was not booked up. His office was empty when we walked in, and his secretary looked up with the air of a salesclerk about to pounce on a new customer.

I introduced the two of us. "We're not patients, but we'd like to talk to Dr. Boland, if he has a minute. I was a good friend of Kevin Cassidy's."

"Oh." She hesitated. "What was it you wanted to talk about?"

"Just the last few days of Kevin's life. It's hard when someone you love dies, and you're far away and can't get there in time." I tried to make it sound as though we would have come rushing across the Atlantic if we'd only known.

"Oh," she said again, sounding doubtful. I could see why. "Well, I suppose—"

"Amy, could you get me Mrs. Cooper's file?"

"Oh, Doctor, these people want to talk to you about Mr. Cassidy. They say they're friends of his." Her voice sounded so dubious I thought I'd better get my two cents' worth in.

"I've been a patient of Dr. Foley's for years," I said with my highest-wattage smile. "He tells me you attended Kevin in his last illness. He speaks very highly of you, by the way." I've always felt that a little insincerity in a good cause doesn't really count as a lie.

"Yes, well, come in." His tone was grudging, but he opened the outer office door and let us in.

Doc Foley had described him as a young man. Young is a relative term. This man was in his mid-forties at the most generous estimate. He was tall and thin, with drooping shoulders and sparse pepper-and-salt hair.

"I don't know what I can tell you," he said when we were seated in his cheerless office. "He was ninety-six years old. He got pneumonia, and we couldn't cure him. It's hardly an uncommon story." His manner was stiff and wary.

"I'm sure you did the best you could," I said gently.

"Are you?" He fixed me with a gimlet gaze. "Or did you come here to try to ferret out what I did wrong? How I could let such a wonderful man die? How I could let a simple case of pneumonia get out of hand? Et cetera, et cetera."

His hands worked restlessly.

"Good Lord, I even made a house call! How many doctors do you know who do that nowadays?"

"Yes, I'd heard that, and I wondered about it."

"He was a very old man, and he called Doc's office saying he wasn't feeling so good. But Doc was away, and Cassidy didn't have a way in to town. My practice wasn't exactly booming, so I thought I might as well run out.

"I tried to talk him into coming to the hospital right then! His chest was bad, really bad. But he said he just wanted some drugs, hated hospitals. It was another two days before he showed up in the emergency room.

"Do you know what rumors can do to a medical practice? Especially in a small town? I've had one cancellation after another since that damn case. Nobody comes right out and says anything, of course. No, they just suddenly have reasons why they have to break their appointments, and they don't schedule another one. Or they just don't show up, don't even bother to call. So if you're trying to dig up some dirt, let me just tell you that nobody could have cured that man. He'd let it go for too long before he came in, and I don't care if he was a combination of the pope and Mother Teresa, there was nothing anybody could have done!''

He was shouting by the time he finished. I was too surprised to reply, and Alan wisely let the silence stretch itself for a moment before opening his mouth.

''Actually,'' he said, ''we're not particularly interested in his death—or not the manner of it, at any rate. We had heard that he had some accidents in the last few months of his life, and simply wondered if any of them could have contributed to the pneumonia.''

The restless hands slowed, stopped. Dr. Boland moistened his lips. ''Sorry. I—sorry. Stupid of me.''

He shook his head and closed his eyes.

''Accidents?'' Alan prompted.

The doctor pulled himself together. ''There was nothing in his record. I remember that for certain, because when Doc Foley got back to town, he mentioned something that made me go back and check.''

The ankle. I exchanged a look with Alan.

''However, the patient apparently had no idea how he'd contracted pneumonia, and you're right. Certain kinds of falls, or prolonged bed rest, especially in the elderly, can lead to pulmonary edema. Fluid in the lungs,'' he added in concession to laymen. ''So I had him X-rayed pretty completely. I did find a couple of cracks and chips here and there—no broken bones, and no real indication of how old the other injuries were. By the time I thought of asking him, he was in a coma.'' He shrugged. ''Not that it made a nickel's worth of difference, really, how he contracted the disease. It's just neater if we know.''

''Yes, I can see that.'' I was ready to ask a few questions now. "What about any other diseases? Flu, or anything like that? I got the idea from one of his neighbors that he didn't go out much, so I wondered if he'd bothered about a flu shot."

"Not that I know. But it would be in his record, and of course that's still in Foley's office. What does it matter to you, anyway?"

"I just find it hard to understand how such an active, healthy man could get sick and die so quickly, that's all." I held up my hand. "And no, I'm *not* blaming you. It's a kind of denial, I guess. Did he—did he suffer at all?"

Dr. Boland relaxed at last. "No. You can rest assured about that. Pneumonia is one of the easiest ways for the old to go. They just slip into a coma and eventually stop breathing. Pneumonia is sometimes called 'the old man's friend,' you know."

"I know. That, at least, makes me feel better." I signaled to Alan with my eyes. We stood. "Thank you for your time, Doctor. I'm sorry we upset you."

"No, it was my fault. I've gotten used to taking offense when none is intended. I shouldn't have blown my top."

With mutual assurances that it didn't matter a bit, Alan and I slipped out of the office. But once we were well out of earshot, he murmured, "Another one who's belligerent."

TEN

"THE GREAT-NIECE," I said as we drove away. "She's the last one on the list, until we get to his friends. And maybe we can get a lead on some of the closest of them tonight. Did I remember to tell you we're going out to dinner?"

"No. Who is it this time? Another suspect?"

"No, this is the night for Frank's old dean. He is, of course, in the biology department, so he could be a part of that conspiracy you talked about earlier."

"Ah, yes. Perhaps I should go prepared to make a citizen's arrest. Except for the minor detail that I am not a citizen. Meanwhile, how are we to find the great-niece? Do we even know her name?"

"No, but I know how to find out." I steered the car to a parking space. "I'll be back in a minute."

It took a little longer than that, but I came back triumphant. "Mary Alice Harrison, 702 North Maple."

"Very well, I am duly impressed. Do you explain your magic tricks, or leave your audience baffled?"

"This is the newspaper office. The *Hillsburg Herald.* I looked up Kevin's obituary in the morgue. Small-town newspapers are obliging, and their obituaries are very complete, with addresses and everything. They have to fill up the paper somehow."

"Unfair! Your local knowledge gives you too much of an advantage over Inspector Plod."

I found the house without much trouble. Alan was right; the residential areas had changed much less than the business districts. Maple Street flaunted its name in a gorgeous display of reds and golds.

"There are," Alan said admiringly, "some things that you Yanks do better than we do. Our autumn is a drab affair by comparison."

"The color is early this year. They must have had a cold summer and a very early frost."

I had worried that we might not find Mrs. Harrison at home, but the shrill cries of children at play in the backyard reassured me. The house was nice enough, a sort of neo-Colonial, but it wasn't the sort where one would expect to find a nanny. Mom was certainly at home. I rang the bell.

And rang it again. Alan raised his eyebrows. "Shall we try the back garden?"

"Oh, of course, she's probably out playing with the kids."

Sure enough, when we moved to the fence at the side of the house, we could see a woman of about thirty sitting in a lawn chair, keeping an eye on two children of about three and five who were playing on an elaborate wooden swing set. She looked tired. She also looked very pregnant.

I tapped on the gate. "Mrs. Harrison?"

She frowned. "Sort of." The younger child—boy?— fell off the swing and started to wail. "You're okay, Jackie. Come on over here, and I'll kiss it well."

The toddler clambered into her lap. "Oof. Careful, kid. Skeezix here doesn't like being kicked. He'd rather do the kicking himself. There, now, is that better?" She kissed the little boy's elbow and cuddled him fondly. He tucked his head into her shoulder, put a thumb in his mouth, and gazed at us. His sister, jealous or uneasy, ran over and hugged her mother's arm, also gazing steadily.

"Something I can do for you?"

I hesitated. "It looks as if you have your hands full there. I wanted to talk to you about your uncle. You don't know me, but Kevin and I were great friends. But maybe I should come back another time—"

Something in the woman's face hardened. The little boy started to wail again. "Sue, why don't you take Jackie in the house and give him some juice?"

"Can I have some, too? And a cookie?"

At the magic word, Jackie sat up, injuries forgotten. Mrs. Harrison sighed. "Yes, but only one. I'm trusting you, now."

"Okay, Mommy. Here, Jackie." Full of self-importance, Sue held out her hand to her little brother and led him into the house.

At a gesture from Mrs. Harrison we opened the gate and went into the backyard. She didn't invite us to sit down. "Okay. We've only got a minute. They can deal with a cookie in less time than it takes a vacuum cleaner. What do you want?"

Her voice was as tired as her face.

"Are you sure you don't want us to come back later? Maybe when your husband's home to help with the kids?"

"My husband won't be home. He's decided he'd rather be married to a piece of fluff from his office who doesn't want kids. So say what you want to say and have done with it."

What I wanted to say after that little outburst was

good-bye. I could have kicked myself. I'd forgotten Jerry's scuttlebutt about Mrs. Harrison's marital problems, and now I'd destroyed any chance for friendliness. But we were here. I might as well stick it out, and then maybe I wouldn't have to invade this bitter woman's privacy again.

"It isn't all that important, really, and I'm sorry to bother you. I've just been trying to talk to people, his neighbors and so on, who were close to your uncle in his last weeks. It makes me feel less guilty about not keeping in close touch."

"I know who you are," said Mrs. Harrison slowly. "You talk kind of English. You're that woman who moved away, the one he left his money to, aren't you?"

"Umm—he did leave me a small bequest, yes, but—"

"Well, it's more than he did for me. I went to his lawyer and asked. I needed money, and I thought maybe I could get an advance from my inheritance. That's when I found out there wasn't any inheritance. So why should I care about making you feel better?"

"Mrs. Harrison, I'm sorry that you resent me. I never meant to do you any harm, and if I can lend you—"

"Don't call me Mrs. Harrison! I'm taking my own name back. And don't patronize me. My husband's left me, I'm almost due, and I've lost my job. They called it 'downsizing,' but I know it was because I've got kids. They figured I'd miss too much work. So now I've got to try to find something else, and nobody'll even talk to me until after the baby's born. My dear ex doesn't pay his child support, and I could have used that money he gave you, but forget it. It's a drop in the bucket, anyway."

"But surely, Mrs.—umm—surely if you needed money that badly, you could have asked your uncle."

"He was my great-uncle. Not all that close. Anyway, he'd already given me money, and I felt bad about asking for more. Loans, he called them. He was a great guy, don't get me wrong, and I was sorry when he died. But he'd been so generous when he was alive…. I knew he didn't have much left, but I thought he might've left me something, and I could've taken it, now that it wouldn't leave him short."

The children reappeared, squabbling fiercely. Sue had a bright red stain on her pink T-shirt. "Mommy, Jackie squirted his juice at me! He did it on purpose, too!"

Mrs. Harrison, or whatever she was calling herself now, went back to mothering, her voice gentle again as she dealt with her children.

I looked at Alan. He nodded. We went back to the car and drove off. I doubt if mother and children even noticed.

WE BARELY HAD TIME to change clothes and make it to the dean's house a fashionable fifteen minutes late. There was no time to compare ideas or write down the information we had gained.

"A lot to think about" was Alan's only comment.

"We'll sleep on it and get back to work tomorrow."

Dean Elliot and his wife were charming people, but a good deal more formal than the Foleys. We chatted about inconsequentials over dinner. Kevin's name didn't come up until we were sipping brandy in the elegant living room.

"I'd like to make a toast," said the dean. "Or perhaps two of them. First, to friends, old and new." He lifted his glass and nodded gracefully, first to me, then to Alan. "And second, to two very fine scientists and valued colleagues, Frank Martin and Kevin Cassidy."

If I hadn't suspected what was coming, I'd have disgraced myself with tears. Frank's name, heard unexpectedly, could still do that to me. Fortunately, I'd heard the dean do this sort of thing before, so I was able to lift my glass composedly and join in the toast. I felt Alan's glance, though, and knew that he knew what I was thinking. He usually did.

"How well did you know Kevin, Dean?" I asked when I had put my glass down. I'd had more than enough to drink.

"Not well, really, except by reputation. He'd retired before I came to Randolph, but of course he continued his experimental work until the last few years of his life, so I came across him now and again in the labs. A truly brilliant microbiologist."

"Frank always said Kevin had the finest mind he'd ever come across. I don't know a lot about the technical aspects of microbiology, of course, but I do know that Kevin could argue circles around anybody, on almost any subject, and leave his opponents laughing when he'd finished demolishing them. We used to have some wonderful parties in the old days, when he was at the top of his form."

"That, I always think," said Helen Elliot, "is one of the saddest things about growing old. Kevin was still sharp as a tack, right up to the end, but he'd gotten out of the habit of going places. He used to come to our parties, too, years ago, but I hadn't seen him in, oh, two or three years, I expect. I think his best friends had died off, one by one, and he didn't make new ones once he left the university."

"The isolation of age," said Alan, nodding. "I imagine that's what killed him, in the end. He became ill, and there was no one to get him to a doctor in time.

Although we have been hearing about some accidents that might have caused the pneumonia.''

"Accidents? How could an accident cause pneumonia?'' Helen asked.

"Staying in bed too much, I expect, dear,'' said the dean. "Not good for anyone, and very bad for the elderly, whose lungs don't work too efficiently anyway. But I never heard that Kevin was prone to accidents.''

"We'd lost touch, both of us,'' said Helen, shaking her head. "I felt so badly about it when it was too late.''

We commiserated with each other over our mutual feelings of guilt, and then changed the subject to something more cheerful. I drank some more brandy, against my better judgment, and let Alan drive us home.

We slept late the next morning under the influence partly of the brandy and partly of the weather. The beautiful spell we'd been having had broken during the night. We woke to dismal clouds and steady rain, and went back to sleep again.

When I finally roused myself, I took a couple of aspirin for my headache and made coffee in the little appliance provided by a thoughtful management. I poured a cup for Alan and handed it to him in bed.

"Here. Restorative.''

Alan, thank heaven, is not the chatty sort first thing in the morning. I surface slowly, myself, and cannot abide bright cheeriness until I've had at least one cup of coffee.

"Not a very pleasant day'' was Alan's first comment, when we had both ingested sufficient caffeine to be more or less human.

"No.'' I yawned hugely. "I'm sorely tempted to crawl back into bed.''

"We-ell...," said Alan, patting the pillow next to him and giving his best imitation of a leer.

"Not this morning, love, I've got a headache."

And then I heard what I'd said, and we broke into giggles at the stale old line, and by the time we recovered, we were both wide awake.

"Very well, what *shall* we do today? I categorically refuse to go out. And I may say, by the way, that I am sorely disappointed by this rain. You, my dear, quite clearly gave me to understand that the weather in America is always fine."

"Almost always. Except in the fall, of course. And the spring. And sometimes in summer. And then of course in winter we get some snow, and a fair amount of sleet. But most of the time, it's beautiful."

"Anything you say, dear. To get back to the subject at hand—"

"I think it's time to put what we've got in logical order and see if there's a pattern. We've been running around talking to everybody we can think of. Let's see if we've accomplished anything."

So we ordered bagels and juice from room service along with more coffee, and for what was left of the morning we attacked the notebook, making additions and corrections and trying to make sense of what we knew or surmised. At the end of it we had a table with everything neatly laid out in columns: name, means, motive, opportunity, other salient factors. The neatness was the primary virtue of the thing.

"There just isn't anything to get hold of!" I slammed the pen down on the table. "Jerry's a menace to society, according to the police chief. Mrs. Schneider's trying to save society, according to Mrs. Schneider. That ghastly preacher thinks Kevin was beyond the pale because he was Catholic. His attorney is keeping her mouth tight shut, and his doctor is paranoid. And the great-niece, Mrs. Whatever—or Ms. Whatever, I suppose—is bitter about Kevin's will, but she's also bitter about life in general. There's not a teaspoonful of hard evidence in the whole mess!''

"Oh, I think you're being a trifle too negative about that. Look at all these people who had a financial interest, of one kind or another.''

I looked. ''Mrs. Schneider?''

''She said he contributed to her cause.''

''So she did. Okay, so everyone except the doctor had money from him, in one way or another. So what?''

''And the attorney.''

''I think she did, too. She acted odd when the loans came up. Of course she didn't say anything, but I got the distinct impression that she knew something personal about that whole loan business. What I don't see is why you keep harping on it.''

''I'm not sure, myself. It seems to me to be curious, though, and I like to keep the curious in mind. You know, Dorothy, I think we may be approaching this the wrong way.''

''What do you mean?''

''We've considered it, up to now, as a puzzle to be solved. Find the pieces, arrange them in order, and voilà! The true picture emerges. Or, to put it another way, locate all the clues, interpret them, solve the mystery.''

''What other way is there to think about it?''

''I have the feeling that the answers we're seeking will reveal themselves, if at all, only when we really know Kevin.

''What I mean,'' he went on when I looked about to object, ''is that this crime, if crime there has been, seems to me to revolve, more than any I've ever approached in a long career, around the character of the victim. You knew Kevin for many years, but you'd lost touch of late. I never knew him at all, though I'm beginning to. I think we're both going to have to know him very well indeed before we'll have any idea who might have wanted him dead.''

I considered the matter. ''That's a tall order. I suppose we just go on talking to people, seeing him from as many different points of view as we can?''

''That's the idea.''

''Well, you have a point, but we also need any evidence we can uncover.''

Alan the policeman grinned. ''Of course we do.''

''Well, then, I'd still like to know more about any other accidents Kevin might have had. Do you suppose the hospital would let us see those X rays Dr. Boland mentioned?''

''Probably not, unless we can think of a good reason. Doc Foley might be able to get them for us.''

''We'd have to tell him why.''

''We may, you know, have to take someone into our confidence, and Doc Foley is our best candidate, I think. For one thing, he was out of town when the trouble began, and—you trust him, don't you?''

''With my life. Well, I *have* trusted him with the care of my life, for years. If he isn't trustworthy, I may start wondering whether you are.''

''Very well, then. I must say I had the same impression, but one evening's acquaintance is hardly sufficient to tell. I'm glad of your testimonial. We'll keep him in reserve as a confidante. Meanwhile, I'm hungry. That wasn't much of a breakfast. Suppose we go downstairs and see what they can give us for lunch, and then—do you still have a headache?''

IT RAINED ALL DAY and into the night, but the next morning, Wednesday, dawned clear and cool. I was full of energy.

"Alan, let's go out and see Jerry. Right away, as soon as we've had breakfast. If we get there early enough, he won't offer us anything to eat. And I really do want to ask if he knows anything about accidents, or anything else peculiar that might have happened to Kevin."

"Splendid. And when we've finished there, had we best pack up some things to ship back to England?"

"Heavens! We've only got two more nights here, and I don't want to haul all that stuff somewhere else. I forgot about it. We should have packed yesterday."

"Oh, there's plenty of time. But by all means, let us beard Jerry in his den as soon as possible."

"And we can hit Mrs. Schneider on the way back; she's close. We'd better call first, though. She's so busy, and I don't think she likes people just dropping in."

"What excuse do you plan to use this time?"

"Oh." I thought for a moment. "How about if we wait and call her after we've talked to Jerry? There are lots of pay phones around, what with all that awful development on that side of town. And we can say we were in the neighborhood and wanted to know how the antidevelopment fight was coming. It's perfectly true, too. I really do want to cheer her on. She's taking on the big guys and sticking to her guns. That takes courage."

So, remembering the way Jerry lived, we put on the oldest clothes we'd brought with us and made our way out to the trailer.

I had to find it from Kevin's house. Presumably there

was some sort of drive directly to Jerry's property, so he could get his motorcycle out and get to town, but I had no idea how to find it from the main road. So we approached through the woods as we had done before.

"Darn it," I said as we got to the clearing. "He must not be home. Look at the cats."

There were five or six of them pacing around the trailer, yowling. An orange tabby, a small gray tabby, a beautiful long-haired black, a huge black-and-white specimen of what a friend of mine calls a "Holstein cat"—they were in constant motion, and I lost count. The gray one trotted confidently up to us and started stropping itself against Alan's ankle, mewing loudly in anxious little chirps.

"Oh, Alan, they're hungry, poor things. Jerry must have gone off without feeding them."

"Surely there's plenty of game in the wood."

"Yes, but when they're raised as pampered house cats, they're not always good at catching their own food. I'm disappointed in Jerry. I thought he'd be more responsible than that, even if he is a little peculiar."

Alan picked up the little cat so as not to step on it and walked over to the trailer door. "He might be sleeping off a few beers too many. Can't hurt to knock. And Dorothy, if he isn't home, all is not lost. We could finally get into Kevin's house."

He put the cat down gently and banged on the door. There was no response, but the door swung open. "He hasn't repaired that catch yet."

"Would it be okay to go in and find some cat food, do you think?" I reached down to pet the black cat, who had approached with great dignity and an imperious look. "Jerry wouldn't mind."

"No. Wait." Alan's voice was sharp, curt, official. "Don't come closer, Dorothy."

"What—?" I stopped and swallowed hard. The smell had reached me.

Jerry's trailer hadn't smelled good the first time, but the stench now was infinitely worse. Sickly sweet, catching at the throat... I swallowed again. The smell of rotten meat. Or...

ELEVEN

ALAN WOULDN'T LET ME go inside. He took out a handkerchief to cover his hand, opened the screen, and made a brief reconnaissance before rejoining me.

"I called the police; they're on their way."

"So it is Jerry? And he is…?"

"It is, and he is."

"How did he—" I didn't seem to be able to finish a sentence.

"I don't know, my dear. Not quietly in his bed, however. He's lying in the middle of the floor. There are no obvious signs of violence, but of course I didn't examine the body."

He sounded grim, and for a moment I wondered why. We had barely known Jerry, and death, for a policeman, isn't quite as shattering as for the rest of us.

Then I understood. He wasn't a working policeman anymore. In fact, as far as Indiana was concerned, he never had been. The retired chief constable of Belleshire, with over forty years of experience, was going to have to stand by and watch while somebody else investigated a case of unexpected death. And the somebody else didn't much care for Alan.

"Alan, he was fine when we saw him on Saturday. This is only Wednesday. How long do you think he's been dead?"

"My dear, how would I know? Some time, certainly, from the stench, but it's terribly hot in the trailer. The central heating was blasting away. That would speed the postmortem changes, of course."

I shuddered. "And out here in the woods, with that ramshackle old trailer, I suppose there'll be...insects..."

"If there are, Dorothy, they'll help the process of determining time of death. The life cycles are quite definitive, you know—"

"I know." I've read enough detective fiction to know about maggots, but I certainly didn't want to hear any more about them right now. I was having enough trouble keeping my stomach under control as it was.

The little gray cat came back, rubbing my ankles and purring urgently. I picked her up and cuddled her, but she wriggled free. Love was not what she wanted right now.

"Alan, what are we going to do about the cats? They're starving. There's sure to be food for them in the trailer. I don't suppose, if I was careful not to touch anything—"

"No. For one thing, you don't want to go in there. The odor is really quite unpleasant. For another, you'd corrupt what may be a crime scene, whether you meant to or not. I did, simply by using the telephone. That was unavoidable, but the cats will have to wait."

Well, if Alan, the understated Englishman, said the odor was unpleasant, he meant it was well-nigh unbearable. I was quite content not to enter the horrid little trailer, but the gray cat had another point of view. So did the others. They set up a constant chorus of complaint and petition, accompanied by ankle-weaving and, in the case of the black one, a quick, sharp dig in the calf with an unsheathed claw by way of emphasis.

That did it. "I can't stand it. The poor things! I'm going somewhere to buy cat food. Unless you think I need to stay here."

"I shouldn't think so. Hurry back, because the police will probably want to question you. And don't forget bowls of some sort. You can't use anything at all from the trailer."

I found a new gas station/convenience store near the turnoff from the state highway. They had cat food, probably at a wildly inflated price, but everything here in Indiana was so much cheaper than in England that it seemed almost reasonable. I picked up several cans in different flavors and a bag of dry food. I remembered the bowls, cheap plastic ones, along with some plastic spoons. I even bought a gallon of designer water. I probably wouldn't be allowed anywhere near Jerry's sink.

I was waiting at the checkout counter, my heavy basket weighing down my arm, when a woman walked in and stared at my hat. She looked familiar.

"Don't I know you from someplace?" We spoke together, in almost the same words, and then laughed.

"Oh, I know now. The voice did it. You're that friend of Kevin Cassidy's, the woman from England—"

"Dorothy Martin. From Hillsburg, but lately from England. And you're Mrs. Schneider."

"Hannah, right." She glanced down at my basket. "Have you decided to move back here and acquire a menagerie, or is that a donation to the animal shelter?"

"Neither. It's—oh, yes, sorry." I unloaded the basket on the counter for the clerk. "I'm buying this stuff for Kevin's cats."

"I thought they were all set. Living with that crazy neighbor of his."

"They were, but—wait a minute." I paid for my purchases and picked up the bags. "Unfortunately, Jerry has died—"

She made a shocked noise.

"—so the cats are on their own again. I suppose they'll have to go to a shelter, but for the time being I'm trying to look after them. We were the ones who found Jerry, Alan and I, so I have to get back there to talk to the police and everything—"

"Police!"

"Well, it's an unexpected death. He wasn't sick on Saturday—that's when we met him. And—" I hesitated. How much should I tell her? Then I shrugged mentally. The whole story would be all over town in a day or two, anyway. "—and we're afraid it might not be a natural death. He—I haven't seen him, but Alan says he's lying in the middle of the floor, so—"

"Hmph! Don't know that I'd have expected anything else."

"Yes, well…we were planning to stop and see you later, perhaps, Alan and I, but now I don't know if—"

"You're welcome any time. But do call first."

"I remember. I must go."

The trip had taken longer than I'd planned. By the time I got close to Jerry's trailer (still through the woods), the whole place was surrounded by police cars with flashing lights and blaring radios, and the cats had vanished.

I was annoyed at the hullabaloo. Surely they were making a huge fuss over what might be a very simple matter. And they had terrified the cats.

I stood at the edge of the clearing and called softly, "Here, kitty, kitty." No response. Maybe no one had ever called them "kitty" before, and I didn't know their names. I could just set out the food, of course, but wild animals might eat it before the cats could get a chance. However, I couldn't stand there all day waiting for frightened cats to return. I popped the top off one of the cans.

That's all it took. They appeared, slowly, warily. They jumped every time another call came over the police radio. But hunger is a powerful lure.

I put bowls of dried and canned food on the ground, poured bowls of water, and then trudged into the clearing.

"This is a crime scene, ma'am. I'll have to ask you to stay back." The deputy, or whatever he was, looked at me oddly.

I was wearing the only set of comfort clothes I'd brought with me: old shoes, blue jeans, a red-checked shirt, a sturdy sweater that wasn't exactly new, and one of my favorite hats in bright orange wool for the chilly morning. The hat had pheasant feathers for decoration. I was carrying a large purse with hand-painted cats all over it, a large grocery bag, and a gallon jug of water. I tried not to let my mouth twitch.

"I'm Dorothy Martin. My husband and I found the body. And what makes you think it's a crime scene?"

He ignored the question. "Oh. Right. What's in the bag?"

"Cat food. Empty cans. Somebody had to feed Jerry's cats. Why do you think Jerry's death is a crime?"

The policeman cleared his throat. "Right," he said again. "I'll get the chief."

Alan walked over. He looked unhappy. "Your old pupil has classified me as a suspect."

"A suspect for what? What's happening?"

"Apparently they're not quite satisfied about the death. There is no wound of any kind."

"Darryl told you that?"

"Darryl prefers not to tell me anything, but I have excellent ears, and his men have not been quite as careful as they might be in my presence."

"But he can't possibly think that *you*—what did he say?"

"Very little in words. A great deal in attitude."

"Well, his deputy, or whatever he is, thinks I'm a bag lady. We may end up in the clink together."

"And then what will happen to the cats?" He, too, was trying to play it as a comedy, and I was willing enough to follow the sidetrack.

"Oh, Alan, I can't even think about it! We can't do anything about them ourselves, in a hotel. Nobody will take them in, there are too many of them, and a shelter would—"

"Mrs. Martin." Darryl sounded very official and very unlike the little boy I'd taught in fourth grade. "I'd like to talk to you for a minute. Could you come with me?"

I turned to hand Alan my burdens, but Darryl put his hand on my arm. "Bring them with you, please."

He took me to one of the police cars and climbed into the backseat with me. "It's the only place to sit. Put the bag on the seat, please."

He emptied everything out of the grocery sack. Cans, dirty spoon, everything. Without comment he put out his hand for my purse and emptied it as well. He even opened the jug of water and sniffed it.

"Well, that checks out," he said with a hint of relaxation in his voice. "Now, can you tell me where you were and what you did for the last few days? From Saturday night on, say?"

"Is that when he died? On Saturday?"

Darryl just looked at me.

"Oh, very well. Well, we saw you Saturday afternoon, and when you had to leave, we went back to the hotel for a while. After that I did some shopping—bought some books—and then we spent the evening in, just reading and watching TV. Then, let's see, Sunday." I racked my memory and came up with most of what we did on Sunday and Monday, though I left out the reasons for the many conversations we'd had with possible murder suspects. "Just getting back in touch with my roots," I said firmly. "And yesterday we didn't go out at all. The weather was too bad. We—we spent most of the day just reading, talking...." I hoped he didn't notice the hesitation. I wasn't going to tell a boy I'd met when he was nine years old how we'd spent the early afternoon.

Either he didn't notice, or Alan had already mentioned our amorous activities. "Okay, that checks out, too. Any witnesses for Saturday night or yesterday?"

"Good grief, Darryl, we were alone in our hotel room! We did have dinner at the hotel that night, but after that...and yesterday we had all our meals at the hotel. We were pretty sick of the food by the end of the day, let me tell you. In between meals, though—how could there be witnesses?"

"Right." He made a note. "Thank you, Mrs. Martin. That'll be it, for now, anyway. You'll have to come down to the station later to have your fingerprints taken, since you were in the trailer earlier."

"Darryl." I tried to keep my voice level. "Come off it."

He muttered something.

"You can't seriously consider either of us as suspects! Even if you were sure Jerry was murdered, and I can't imagine what makes you think that at this stage, what conceivable reason would we have to kill him?''

"Motive isn't a very important factor in a police investigation, at least not at first," he said stiffly.

"Darryl!"

I must have sounded like an outraged schoolteacher, because he shifted in his seat and looked embarrassed.

"Okay, maybe I don't think you're very likely. Either of you. In fact, I think—but I have to go by the book. And the fingerprints—since yours will be in there, we have to be able to rule those out."

Especially when a stuck-up English policeman is around. He might just as well have said it aloud. I ignored it and pounced on his unfinished sentence.

"*What* do you think?"

He shook his head, stubbornly.

"Oh, for heaven's sake! Very well, am I allowed to go now?"

He helped me out of the car with more haste than care. I think he was as eager to see me gone as I was to get out of there. Alan and I walked back to our car in silence, but as soon as we were safely inside I exploded.

"Alan, that little twerp—"

He patted my hand. "Don't get upset. He's just doing his job."

"What do you mean, doing his job? He knows perfectly well—"

"No, he doesn't. Not for certain, and a policeman has to be certain. But if it makes you feel any better, he doesn't really think we had anything to do with Jerry's death."

"How do you know?"

"More eavesdropping. Apparently Jerry was involved in a tavern brawl on Saturday night. Blows were ex-

changed. The general feeling is that someone followed
him home and decided to settle the argument perma-
nently.''

"How? You said there were no wounds.''

"The betting is on more whiskey or whatever. A great
deal more.''

"Alcoholic poisoning?''

"It's not unreasonable, actually, given Jerry's habits.
They'll check for time of death, of course. Those insects
you don't like to think about will help. I heard one of
the men talking about calling in 'the bug man,' as he
worded it. No, the theory makes a certain amount of
sense. Except that it doesn't take into account—''

"Exactly.''

There was no need to say any more. Silently, I started
the car, put it in gear, and drove back to the hotel, my
thoughts and emotions churning.

We went up to our room. We took off our sweaters
and hung them up with some care. We sat down.

Finally, I said, "Okay. Do you really think Jerry was
killed because of some Saturday-night brawl?''

There was a long pause. Alan ran a hand down the
back of his neck, adjusted his collar. "No.''

I waited expectantly. He said no more.

"Well?''

"Just that. I don't think he was killed because of a
brawl. I have no reason whatever for that opinion, except
that I don't believe in coincidence.''

Another long pause.

"Alan, we're in a mess.''

"Yes.''

"We're involved in an unexpected death. If we go
around asking questions about Jerry or Kevin, Darryl

will find out, and we'll be in even worse trouble. Do we give up?''

Alan stood up and began to prowl. Suddenly he turned back to me. ''No, I'm damned if we do!''

TWELVE

ALAN ALMOST NEVER swears. I waited while he paced.

"I don't believe in coincidence," he repeated. "Kevin dies, under circumstances that seem perfectly normal—except that he thought he was going to be murdered. We come to town and begin nosing about, and Jerry—his nearest neighbor, the one who perhaps knew more about Kevin's last days than anyone else—Jerry dies, under circumstances that are odd, to say the least.

"Dorothy, it is that fact—Jerry's death—that's convinced me at last. I believe Kevin's letter. I believe that somehow, no matter how impossible it seems, he was murdered. I believe Jerry knew something important, and was murdered to ensure his silence. And I'll be hanged if I'll allow the murderer to get away with it!"

He sat down, took my hand, and let out his breath in an explosive sigh. "I must say I feel better."

"So do I. But what are we going to do about it? We've talked to everybody we can think of and learned precious little. Oh, maybe we're building up that picture of Kevin's life you think is so important, but we don't seem to have gathered much actual evidence. Evidence is what the police are so good at. And we can't talk to Darryl because he's a possible suspect, and besides he's got it in for us."

That produced a small grin. "You can't have it both

ways, you know. Either Darryl is a murderer or he suspects us of being murderers.''

"Oh. You're right. But either way, we can't really tell him anything.''

"No.'' Alan stood up again, rubbed his hand down the back of his neck, and began to pace the small room. "I must say I find it odd at my time of life to be withholding information from the police.''

I'd been doing that sort of thing for quite some time, ever since I took up crime (as in: the investigation of), but I judged it wasn't the moment to say so. "Not only that, but we can't get any information from them, either. That makes it even harder to get anywhere ourselves.''

"But not impossible!'' Alan smacked the table he was passing. "Dorothy, we've got back round to the idea of a confidante—Dr. Foley. We talked about him before. He can't give us the same kind of information that the police could, but he can look up details of Kevin's last illness.''

"And maybe of some of those 'accidents.' Look, I have an idea. I still haven't worked out where we're going on Friday when we have to get out of here. What if I call the Foleys and see if they have room for us, for the weekend anyway? That would give us plenty of time to talk, unless Doc has a bunch of emergencies.''

Alan raised his eyebrows. "Are they such good friends that you can beg a bed on two days' notice?''

"I can ask, anyway. And no, they won't be offended.''

Peggy was delighted. Of course they had room. "We've got that whole guest cottage, you know. And our football company for this weekend pooped out on us, so we were going to have to go alone. To the *Notre Dame* game! Do you have tickets?''

"We do. I had to move heaven and earth and pull every string I could think of, but we've got them. I think they're up in nosebleed territory somewhere. We'll have a wonderful view of the Goodyear blimp."

"No, you won't. We always get four season tickets, and they're almost smack on the fifty-yard line. Oh, this is going to be fun!"

So we made arrangements to arrive late Friday morning. I hung up and turned to Alan.

"So that's that. But Friday's two days away, and Doc may not be home till late in the evening. He works awfully hard. So what do we do in the meantime? I don't want to discuss this with him on the phone at his office. Too many people to listen in, on both ends."

"Hmmm."

"Now don't get that gleam in your eye! How old do you think we are, anyway?"

"Eighteen."

"Getting close to seventy, both of us."

"What does that have to do with it?"

"Nothing at all, you're right. However, don't forget I have a puritan conscience. And right now it's insisting that I find some useful work to do instead of frittering away the rest of the day."

Alan was disposed to argue with the term *frittering,* but in the end he agreed to go with me to see Hannah Schneider.

"I said I would. Who knows? She might just have some useful information for us. Anyway, I rather like the woman. She's got the courage of her convictions."

We called, and learning she'd be home in the afternoon, spent the rest of the morning organizing a large shipment of our "bargain" goods back to England. After

lunch we dressed in somewhat more respectable clothes
and drove out to Hannah's.

She showed us into a large room probably designed,
in the original farmhouse, to be the parlor. Yes, there
was the fireplace at the end, but it was bare and cold.
Hannah obviously used the space as a workroom. A
sturdy table covered with stacks of papers occupied the
center of the floor; a computer and its appurtenances
occupied one wall. Boxes took up most of the rest of
the space except for one newspaper-covered corner,
where a rather dusty antique chest sat in piebald splen-
dor, half dingy mahogany stain, half clean pine.

"That's a nice piece," I commented. "Is your husband refinishing it? I always heard you weren't supposed
to do that to antiques."

"You're not, not if they're worth anything. This one
isn't. It's just an old Sears, Roebuck chest. Mass produced, and filthy when I bought it, but I thought it would
look nice cleaned up. No, my husband's been gone for
years. I work on it myself when I get the time, which
isn't often.

"I hope you don't mind coming in here. It's cleaner
than it looks, and I have to get these fliers addressed.
We're having a big community meeting about the mall
in a couple of weeks, and we want this whole end of
town to know about it."

She sat down at the table and began peeling computer-
printed labels off a sheet and sticking them on folded
leaflets. "Now tell me, what's all this about Kevin's
crazy neighbor? What was his name, Jimmy?"

"Jerry. Jerry what, I don't know. I suppose I will
tomorrow, when I read the paper." That was sad, I
thought suddenly, to learn someone's name only from
his obituary. "We don't know very much, really, except

that he might not have died of natural causes. The police are apparently treating it as a crime, at least for now.''

''But why? How did he die?''

''They don't seem to know,'' said Alan, stepping smoothly on the reply I had been about to make. ''They're making rather a great fuss about it, don't you think, my dear?'' He smiled blandly at me. I closed my mouth and nodded. ''The poor man rather struck me as the sort to meet a sticky end,'' he went on, ''though one couldn't help feeling sorry for him.''

''Hmph! I'm not so sure about that, a man who didn't even look after his property. He probably drank himself to death.''

Darryl's theory. And it would, I thought, be the popular solution. If that was all Hannah had to offer, we were wasting our time.

Alan seemed to have other ideas. ''Mrs. Schneider,'' he said with one of his disarming smiles, ''would you like us to help with your task? It looks an endless job.''

''Sure! Nice of you to offer. Pull up a couple of chairs and make yourself at home. And call me Hannah.''

So we peeled labels and affixed them to hundreds of leaflets while Alan encouraged Hannah to talk about her pet project. Not that she needed much encouragement. We heard arguments and counterarguments, successes and setbacks in the fight to keep the mall, and development in general, out of Hillsburg.

Oh, it was interesting, up to a point. Alan and I are both opposed to mega-anything and in favor of small business. When I said something to that effect, Hannah was off again on a new tack.

''And don't forget that includes the small farmer. What's going to happen to this country when all the arable land is paved over for malls and highways and cities? What are we going to eat? And what's the small farmer going to live on? And don't forget the environmental impact of all those parking lots! We're having a study done to see what oily runoff from the mall and the roads leading to it would do to the streams and, ultimately, to the aquifer beneath this whole part of the country...."

She let us leave at last, armed with a sheaf of the leaflets. "Just leave them lying around at the hotel, or anywhere else you can think of. We're papering the town with them."

"She's right," I said to Alan when we got back to the peace and quiet of our hotel room. "She's absolutely right about everything she says. So why do I feel so numb?"

"Paralysis of the ear, the inevitable result of listening to a fanatic. You might go and see Ms. Carmichael for a few minutes, as an antidote; she says nothing at all most of the time. The message light on the phone is blinking, love. Shall I get it?"

The recorded voice was Darryl's, sounding grim, reminding us to come to the police station and have our fingerprints taken.

"I suppose we'd better do it." I sighed. "I'd rather sit and listen to Hannah for another two hours, and that's saying something."

The actual fingerprinting wasn't bad, when we got to the police station. The sergeant who supervised the procedure was courteous and absolutely impersonal, and of course we'd both had it done before and knew the drill.

While we were there, the young officer I'd talked to that morning came in. I smiled and said hello.

For a moment he didn't know who I was, now that I

no longer looked homeless. But then he smiled back. "The cat lady!"

"Oh, good heavens, Alan! I forgot all about the cats again. What's to become of the poor things?"

"Now, ma'am, that's all taken care of. I volunteer for the animal shelter. I've rounded them up. Six of them, right?"

"I'm afraid I don't really know. There were a good many, but they never stayed still long enough to count."

"Well, I found six and took them to the shelter."

"But the people won't—I mean, do they—"

"They never kill a healthy animal. They find homes for all of 'em."

"Oh, what a relief. That was really kind of you." I beamed at him. "Listen, if you'll give me the address of the shelter, I'll take over that food I bought. And I'll make a donation as soon as—"

"Mrs. Martin. Mr. Nesbitt. I'd like to talk to you for a minute."

Darryl stood outside his office, beckoning.

He shut the door, went behind his desk, and sat down, without inviting us to do so. "I've been checkin' around," he said without preamble. "You two've been talkin' to a lot of people. Askin' a lot of questions about the professor. And what I want to know is, why?"

THIRTEEN

I LOOKED AT ALAN. He looked at me. Darryl, I thought in a panic, would have to be a total ignoramus not to know we were trying to hide something. And unfortunately he was quite bright, not at all the idiot policeman so prevalent in classic mystery fiction.

If there is a patron saint of liars, he—or more likely she; women are more creative—came to my aid at that moment. God bless Agatha Christie and all the rest who have given me a devious mind, I thought piously as I tried to produce a blush, gave it up as a bad job, and looked Darryl straight in the eye.

"Well, I didn't intend to say anything to anyone, but—no, Alan, let me finish. I've decided to tell all." I tapped my foot against his in an urgent *Keep still* and took a deep breath. "The fact is, Darryl, I'm writing a book."

Whatever the police chief had expected, it wasn't that. As for Alan, I didn't dare catch his eye.

"Actually, that's what we're doing in Hillsburg. You see, I got this letter from Kevin's lawyer...."

The story was straight right up to the point when we opened the letter from Kevin in Ms. Carmichael's office. It took all my acting skill to keep from thinking about the real content of that letter and getting teary, but I managed it. "And the upshot of it was, Kevin wanted me to write his biography. He had an extraordinary life, you know. But Darryl, you'll keep this under wraps, won't you? Kevin didn't want anybody to know about it until it was published—if it ever is. I've never written anything in my life, of course—well, not for publication, that is."

"So why did he choose you to write his life story? And why was he making such a big deal out of it, keeping it a secret and all?"

Drat the boy! I wished I hadn't worked so hard to instill good sense in my fourth-graders. Darryl was being entirely too intelligent about this.

"Well, I think it's just another example of what a nice person he was. The truth is, I used to try to write a little, and Kevin was the only soul who knew about it. I never even told Frank, but Kevin caught me at it one day in the library, and made me show him what I was working on. It was just some reminiscences, tiny things that had happened over the years, funny things my schoolkids had said and done, that sort of nonsense. Anyway, he said he liked it, it was good, I should try to get it published. Well, I never did, of course, and he used to prod me about it now and then when nobody else was around. This biography project was his way of making sure I got serious about writing."

I paused for breath. "And as for the secrecy...I suppose he didn't want word to get out, in case I fell flat on my face. He wasn't out to embarrass me, after all."

It sounded so reasonable I almost began to believe it myself. Even Darryl looked considerably less skeptical.

"How come you had to go around asking all kinds of questions? Kevin must have left you something to go on, notes or diaries or whatever. He couldn't expect you just to pull it all out of your head. The man lived for ninety-six years, for Pete's sake.''

"Of course he had notes, piles of them, I gather, but none of it would cover the last couple of weeks of his life, and I wanted to get that from people while it's fresh in their minds. Details of a death are important in a biography. Besides, all the notes are at Kevin's house, and I haven't had time to collect them yet. Actually, Alan and I intended to go over there this morning, but we stopped to say hello to Jerry, and of course…''

I trailed off artistically. Darryl fiddled with a ballpoint pen, bouncing first one end and then the other on his desk. Finally he sighed and stood up. "Okay. Keep in touch.''

The interview was apparently over.

"Whew!'' I turned to Alan when we were a block or so away, safely out of both sight and earshot of the police station.

"Indeed.'' His tone was a trifle dry.

"All right, I know you don't like lying to the police. But I couldn't just blurt out the real situation, not with him being a suspect! And this way if we go on asking questions, he'll think it's perfectly normal.''

"Well, it's one approach. And in a way it isn't a lie. We are trying to discover Kevin's life story. One could argue that there are similarities between our quest and that of the biographer.''

"Oh. I suppose that's what put it into my head. And here I was taking credit for making it up all by myself. Alan, this is a mess.''

"The situation is unfortunate, certainly.''

Well, that was Alan at his understated British best.

"What it is, is ridiculous. The whole thing, I mean. Here we are, trying to investigate a couple of murders,

neither getting any help from the police nor giving them
any. Talk about futility! The only thing that makes any
sense at all is to try to get Darryl cleared as soon as we
can. Then we can tell him the whole thing and work
together.''

"If, of course, it's possible to clear him."

I put my hands over my ears. "Don't even say that!
In fact, don't say anything. I feel like my head's stuffed
with cream cheese and I can't think at all. Let's go to a
movie, or something, and forget about it for a while."

Nothing showing at Hillsburg's theaters had much ap-
peal, so we went to a video store and rented several of
my favorite old movies and then stopped at a pizza place
and a liquor store. The evening was an orgy of take-out
pizza, beer, and Bing Crosby. I fell asleep to *Going My
Way.*

In the morning my stomach and head were a little
unhappy about my indulgences of the night before, but
my mind was functioning again.

"Alan, I have an idea."

It was too early. We had just begun our first cups of
coffee. Alan grunted and went on sipping, but I per-
sisted. "His priest, Alan. We've forgotten his priest!"

One eyebrow was elevated a sixteenth of an inch.
"You suspect his priest of murder?"

"No, I—never mind, finish your coffee."

But when he was fully awake and I explained, he
agreed that we should talk to Kevin's priest.

"Obvious, really," he commented. "A man Kevin apparently trusted, since he was not on the list of suspects,
a man in whom he might have confided—"

"Hah! You didn't think of it, either!"

"I admit it. Full marks to you, Dorothy. Do you know
him?"

"I used to. He's a lovely man. If it's still the same one. If they haven't gotten in some kid. At least it won't be a woman, not with the Romans." I was still cross about what they'd done to my church.

It was a beautiful morning, October at its loveliest. Brilliant orange and gold leaves drifted to the ground in a light breeze. The Victorian spire of St. Peter's, with its scalloped red shingles and gilded cross, stood out against the bright blue sky as if etched. Even the rectory looked pleasant, its brown brick ugliness hidden by a riot of autumn-painted ivy. We rang the bell.

Yes, said the housekeeper, Father Kennedy was still the pastor at St. Peter's. Yes, he was at home. And if we wouldn't mind waiting a minute or two?

When Father Kennedy appeared, he had changed so little I felt tears start. His blue Irish eyes were just as alert as ever, his smile just as warm. I blew my nose and touched the handkerchief furtively to my eyes. Here, praise the Lord, was something, someone, who hadn't changed in any fundamental way, beyond the normal weight of aging and pastoral cares.

He remembered me. I introduced Alan and we settled down in the rather stuffy and overcrowded office.

"Well now, Mrs. Martin, what can I do for you? Not decided to convert, have you? Leave Henry the Eighth's wicked ways?"

It was his old joke. I smiled broadly, more broadly than the little sally deserved, just because of its familiarity. "No, but you can give us some information, if you will. It's about Kevin Cassidy."

"Ah." His face changed. "Dear old Kevin. My oldest parishioner, you know. He's sadly missed." He looked at me keenly, expectantly.

I took a deep breath. "Father Kennedy, this is going

to sound completely crazy, but Kevin thought somebody was trying to kill him. He left a letter asking me to look into it. And I thought you might know if he'd had any odd accidents in his last few months. There must have been *something* to make him suspicious. Unless, of course, he was just—just senile.''

''No.'' The monosyllable sat there in the room, a stone thrown into a pool of silence. ''I wondered when someone would come to me about this.''

The simple remark took my breath away. ''Then— you *knew?*''

''Oh, yes.'' The priest paused. ''I think I'd better tell you the whole story.'' He settled himself comfortably. ''Will you have some coffee? Or tea? This is going to take a little while.''

We accepted tea. I would be making trips to the bathroom the rest of the morning, but I felt I needed the moral support.

''It began,'' said Father Kennedy, ''or rather I first heard about it, last April. Kevin fell down the front steps of his house and sprained his ankle.''

''Yes, we heard about that one. Doc Foley happened to find out. Apparently Kevin never went to him about it, but then that was the way he was.''

''And often I berated him about it. A man his age ought to look after his health, I'd tell him. But when he came to see me that day, it wasn't his health he wanted to talk to me about.

''Just after Easter, it was. He came here, said he wanted to talk. I was a little surprised. He'd made his Easter confession, and I couldn't imagine…well, he sat here, right in that very chair, Mrs. Martin, and told me he thought someone was trying to murder him.''

He shook his head. "I confess, for just a few minutes I thought he'd lost it. But then he began to tell me.

"That accident, falling down the steps, was just the most recent in a whole series. There'd been his car, first of all."

"Oh, then he *was* still driving."

"He had been. And reasonably well, for someone as old as that. But one day, about a year ago it'd be now, he was driving along that back road of his, and his brakes failed."

I made a shocked noise.

"Yes. There might have been a terrible accident, but he was driving very slowly. He'd slowed still more, for a curve, or he'd tried to, but nothing happened. Well, there was no other traffic, and he had the presence of mind to run the car into a bank at the side of the road. He wasn't hurt, shaken up was all, but the car was fairly well beat up."

"Did he have a mechanic look at the brakes?"

"No, he'd decided then and there that he wouldn't drive anymore. He just had them come and haul the car away, and he never mentioned the brakes to anyone until he told me."

"It must have left him very isolated, not having a car way out there in the country."

"He got a tricycle."

I choked on my tea, and Father Kennedy chuckled.

"Oh, yes, he made quite a picture, pedaling along. It looked very much like an overgrown child's toy, except for being chain driven like a bicycle. The three wheels made it much more stable than a bike, and he didn't need to pedal as fast. Of course, it wasn't much good to him when the weather was bad, but he managed to get to the grocery store when he needed to, get in to town for mass, that kind of thing. His house isn't really that far out, you know. He got along just fine until the tricycle was stolen."

I shook my head sadly. "Things like that never used to happen in Hillsburg."

"They still don't, not often. Kids' bikes, yes. But who'd have any use for an adult tricycle? Anyway, it was the only one in town, and everyone recognized it. Nobody could possibly have used it, not around here. But stolen it was, and boldly, too. From in front of the pet store, in broad daylight. He'd come to town for some cat litter, and when he came out of the store, the trike was gone.

"He couldn't take his purchase home, of course, not without his transportation; the bag was too heavy. But it seemed there was no one around to drive him just then, so he said he'd collect the stuff later, somehow, and he started to walk home. Three miles, and it was a blustery March day, not terribly cold, but with a wind you could stand up against.

"Fortunately, I happened to be driving that way. I saw him and gave him a ride. I scolded him about walking on such a day, but he just glowered at me. Never said a word about the theft; I learned about that later. I think he felt like a fool for letting such a thing happen. Silly, of course, but he had his pride, and a temper, too, you know."

"I do know. An Irish temper," I added.

"And what would ye be meanin' by that?" he demanded in an exaggerated brogue.

But I'd heard the act before. "The sort that's like an April day, thunder and lightning one minute and soft sunshine the next. Your definition, as I recall."

"And me own words used against me!" He twinkled

at me for a moment and then sobered again. "You do see the implication, don't you? Of the theft?"

I saw, all right. "Someone hoped that his heart would give out, walking that far against the wind. Or that he'd get sick. That he'd get pneumonia. But he didn't—not that time. When did you say this happened?"

"Mid-March sometime. I don't recall exactly. I do know he never went for a long walk again. After the tricycle incident—and mind you, I thought it was nothing more than simple theft—I put my foot down and absolutely forbade him to gad about on his own. I didn't like to do it, and Kevin hated the idea like poison. No one wants to lose his independence, but I made him see, at last, that he was taking suicidal risks. The church frowns on suicide, you know. So he gave in, and we organized a schedule at St. Peter's. Someone phoned him every day to see if he needed to go anywhere or have anything brought to him."

"Doc Foley said he was trying to convince Kevin to hire some help around the house."

"Yes, we both were. Everyone knew the volunteer routine wouldn't work forever. He was getting frail; we worried about him falling and not being able to get help. That was another thing. His phone kept going out, and when the repairman would come, he'd never find anything wrong. There was a little fire once, too, one of the times when the phone wasn't working."

I gasped.

"Yes. Oh, Kevin managed to put it out himself. Didn't do much damage. And eventually he got a cellular phone. But even so, it all added up to a dangerous situation. I'd talked to Doc about a live-in housekeeper, even home health care, but Kevin was fighting tooth and nail against it. In the end, of course…'' He held up his hands and shrugged.

''Father, do you think…was his death natural, or… not?''

He thought for a long time, looking at the crucifix on the wall. ''I don't see how it could have been anything but natural. He was lucid at first, you know, and of course I visited him in the hospital. He swore to me he hadn't taken any long walks. He'd had a flu shot, and hadn't been anywhere with lots of people to get exposed to bugs, except to mass, of course. And no one in the parish had pneumonia at the time, or even a serious cold.''

There was more to come; I could feel it. At last he raised his head and turned his bright blue eyes on me. ''No, I don't see how his death could have been anything but natural. That's why I haven't been to the police. And yet, as I hope for heaven, I'm sure that it wasn't. I firmly believe my old friend was murdered, and I'll pray every day that you find out who did it.''

FOURTEEN

"HE'S ANOTHER ONE."

"Another what?" I grabbed Alan's arm as I stumbled over an unexpected curb in the middle of the campus. "What are you talking about?"

"Another of your 'nice people.' You assured me that most of the inhabitants of Hillsburg fell into that category, and I was a trifle skeptical at first. But Father Kennedy fits the description. And the police officer who took the time to make certain the cats were safe. And the young woman at the courthouse."

"Yes, well, I've found out lately that there are quite a few of the other kind, too. And one of them killed Kevin."

Alan cleared his throat, but I rushed on before he could say anything.

"Oh, I know you'll say we still don't have any evidence, and we don't. But we know now, for sure."

"Actually," he said mildly, "what I was about to say was that we now have a good deal of evidence. We know that certain things happened. When we can determine exactly when and how they happened, we'll be a good deal further on."

"But that's just what we can't do! We can't go around asking people exactly when Kevin's brakes failed, or when his tricycle was stolen. Those are police kinds of

questions. And we can't ask Darryl, because he might
be the one.''

I started waving my hands in the air. "Alan, this is
so frustrating! I feel like Harriet Vane in *Gaudy Night*.
She couldn't investigate the Oxford mess properly, because any of the dons might have been the culprit.''

"You'll manage," said Alan soothingly. "You've
dealt with sticky situations before and learned the truth.''

"But that was in England!" I was almost shouting. I
looked around. No one was paying any attention to us,
but I lowered my voice. "I'm a stranger there, or at least
an eccentric American who doesn't count. People will
talk to me. It's entirely different here! This is the town
where I grew up, and most people know me. Even the
ones who don't can at least find out all about me if they
want to, and they certainly won't talk if they have anything to hide. Oh, Alan, it's so stupid, but I can't seem
to accomplish anything here on my own turf. And Kevin
was counting on me!''

My voice had risen to a wail again. Alan steered me
to a bench and sat down with me, his arm around my
shoulders.

"My dear, I think we need a little distance from all
this. It's not like you to lose your sense of proportion.
Regardless of one's belief system, it's certain that Kevin
is no longer troubled about who killed him. One way or
the other, he's beyond worry. The concern is ours now.
Our sense of justice and your love for Kevin demand
that we continue the pursuit. But not, I think, just now.
It's a splendid day. Haven't you some favorite haunt we
could explore, just for a treat?''

I leaned back against his sturdy arm and sighed. "I'd
feel like I was lying down on the job.''

"Come, now. There's no hurry, you know. Evidence

isn't going to vanish now. Most of it is already gone by this time. If Kevin's death is to be solved, it will be solved not by the cigarette ash or the incriminating footprint but by"—he tapped his temple meaningfully—"the little gray cells."

I giggled. Alan wasn't made to play Poirot; he's way too big and way too British. "Oh, I suppose you're right. And very good for me, my love. I do get carried away, don't I?"

"Just a trifle, now and again."

"Well, then. Let me think. Clifty Falls is only about half an hour away. That's a state park just outside Madison that Frank and I used to love, especially in the fall. Or there's Madison itself. It's a beautiful little town with lots of nice old houses. Well, old by American standards. Victorian. They do a tour of them every year just about this time."

"Right." He stood and pulled me up. "We'll make a day of it. Do you want to change clothes?"

We ended up in the tiger sweatshirts. They were just right for Clifty Falls, which was cool in the shade. The sun sifted down through russet and gold leaves, making dappled patterns on the forest floor. We wandered the trails almost alone, the heavy park traffic had vanished with the passing of summer. I kicked through drifts of fallen leaves, listening to the crackle and smelling the sharp, dry perfume. "I feel about ten years old," I told Alan. "It's all I can do not to run and jump in a big pile of them."

We eventually found most of the cataracts that give the park its name, climbing steep sets of wooden steps up or down to vista points. At last, tired and sated, we stopped for a rest.

"It's a lovely place, Dorothy. A bit like parts of Scotland." Alan had found a patch of sunshine and was sitting in the cushiony fallen leaves, his back against an oak tree. "I can understand why it's a favorite spot."

"Mmm. Funny you should mention Scotland. This place is entirely different from Iona, but it provides the same sort of solace to the spirit."

"It's the quiet, I think."

A waterfall not far away provided a constant rush of background noise. A squirrel overhead in the oak tree chattered angrily at us, a blue jay jeered from the top of a white pine, and all the sparrows in the world, congregated in nearby bushes, tweeted and twittered their eternal soprano gossip. I smiled and agreed. "Nice and quiet."

We sat in the noisy quietness, occupied with our own thoughts. Mine inevitably turned to our puzzle, and my peace of mind began to seep away.

"What is it, my dear?" asked Alan at last.

"Hmm?"

"You sighed."

"I did?"

"Deeply. A long, gusty, nobody-knows-the-trouble-I've-seen sigh."

I did it again, resentfully. "I was thinking about Kevin."

Alan pushed himself away from the tree trunk and clasped his arms around his knees. "Feeling a bit sorry for yourself, are you?"

"Alan!"

"Dorothy, you've been moping about ever since we arrived in Hillsburg. Don't you think it's about time you told me about it?"

"I have not been moping! Well, maybe a little, but…"

Alan waited.

My fingers found an acorn and began to peel off the close-fitting cap. "It's childish, I suppose. I—this isn't home anymore!" My chin quivered. I gave my serious attention to the acorn, peeling off one thin strip of papery cap, then another. "I thought," I said when I was sure my vocal cords wouldn't betray me, "that things would be the same, that people would be the same, that I would—would fit in here, the way I used to." I threw away the acorn, now denuded, and started on another.

"You also thought," said Alan gently, "that you would dazzle your friends with your English husband and stories about your detective expertise. Instead you find yourself—what? Rejected?"

"No," I said shortly. Alan was trying to help. I would try to be fair. "Not rejected, exactly. Just—set aside. Unimportant. Not in the scheme of things anymore. And also—ineffectual would be the word, I suppose."

"You think you've accomplished nothing to solve Kevin's murder?"

"Well, have I?"

"Of course you have, and if you'd let your mind dwell for five minutes on the case instead of on your hurt feelings, you'd know it."

I glared at him. He reached over and took my hand.

"Put down that silly object you're so busily shredding and listen to me. You've let your feelings overcome your good sense, my dear. You've been bombarded by conflicting emotions ever since you arrived in this country. Outrage at the physical changes in your old environment, shock at the changes others perceive in you, grief at Kevin's death, frustration at your inability instantly to solve a murky problem. I've watched your self-confidence erode, day by day, despite the fact that you've kept doggedly working away at your puzzle. Now, my love, it's time you snapped out of it.

"Let's take a look at what we've learned. We know, with reasonable certainty, that Kevin was not suffering from paranoia. That string of accidents Father Kennedy related can't be sheer coincidence."

"We can't prove that."

"We can't prove anything at this stage. But we have enough evidence to formulate a theory. Proof can come later. We also know a little, not enough but something, about Kevin's life shortly before he was killed. We know he had sufficient patience to listen to the execrable Pastor Whatever-His-Name-Is, and the wit to give him money to get rid of him. We know how other people reacted to him. We're building up a picture, and we know where the holes are in that picture. Furthermore, we have accomplished this in less than a week, working entirely alone, not only without official help but in the face of considerable official opposition."

He got to his feet and pulled me up after him. "Have I convinced you?"

I smiled, somewhat ruefully. "You've convinced me. I'll be buying medals next to pin on both of us. I've been acting like an idiot, haven't I?"

"Perhaps a bit overwrought at times, that's all. Now, if you love me, tell me where we can find some lunch. I understand there's a lodge in the park."

"There is, and it's nice, too, but very popular. We probably couldn't get in, and I have a better idea, anyway. You like seafood, and there's a nice place in Madison down by the river. The Key West Shrimp House."

"Key West? Isn't that in Florida?"

"Yes. Don't ask me why they call it that. But they have good shrimp, and terrific catfish, and a great salad bar with a mashed potato salad the like of which I've never tasted anywhere else.''

Alan laughed. "Americans have the oddest ideas about food. Mashed potatoes do not comprise my idea of salad, but I'm always ready for a new experience. Lead on, MacDuff.''

I was suddenly starved, too. It is extraordinary how heartening it can be to have the man you love give you a good talking-to. With rather overdone panache and at too great a speed, I drove the hilly, curvy road from the newer part of town on top of the bluff down to Madison proper. A few more blocks, and we were at the foot of Broadway. I pulled the car up and pointed, as proudly as if I'd invented it, at the great river a few feet away.

"The Ohio.''

Broad, beautiful, apparently placid, it flowed past the lovely little park that had graced the riverfront for the past few years. As we watched, a long string of barges moved slowly past, pushed by a tugboat that seemed much too small for the job.

"I've loved this river all my life," I said softly. "It's one of the great rivers of this country, you know. Of the world, really. It flows from Pittsburgh down to the Mississippi, and then on down to the Gulf of Mexico. Navigable all the way. The big riverboats used to carry passengers and freight this way until the railroads came along. The barge traffic is still important, though, and there are two or three fancy pleasure boats still, the *Delta Queen* and the *Mississippi Queen* and one or two others. They call here in summer, right here at this landing. I've always wanted to take that trip, all the way down to the Gulf.''

"Perhaps we will someday." Alan took my hand and

smiled, and we sat and watched the river flow past, jes' rollin' along.

A big fish leaped out of the water and splashed back again. Alan laughed. "That big fellow looks good enough to eat. Which reminds me..."

We walked back up Broadway to the Key West Shrimp House, and there we were immediately brought back to our problem. Straight in front of us sat Hannah Schneider with five or six other women. She was deep in conversation, but she looked up and waved at us.

"Antimall committee?" I asked with a smile, gesturing to the group.

She laughed. "No, but you're close. I'm in Tri Kappa, you know, and they roped me into the Tour of Homes committee this year. It's all in the interest of preservation. We're just settling the last-minute details. It's next weekend; are you and your husband coming?"

"We wouldn't miss it, would we, Alan?"

"No, indeed. Where does one obtain tickets?"

"At the Lanier mansion; that's where the tour begins. Not this coming weekend, you know, but next—the thirteenth, fourteenth, and fifteenth, ten to four. Come early; the lines get long in the afternoon."

She turned back to her meeting, and we were shown to a table in a corner of the room. I tried to concentrate on my food, but I couldn't help thinking about our problem.

"What do you think is our next step?" I asked eagerly, once Alan had eaten enough to be interested in talking.

He looked around cautiously, but the room was full of conversation to cover ours. "We're planning to talk to Dr. Foley tomorrow."

"Yes, but until then!"

"Unless inspiration strikes, we wait."

"But—but I thought it was important to act as quickly as possible in a murder case."

Alan nearly choked on his catfish. When he recovered, he spoke patiently. "The first twenty-four hours are critical, certainly, but once that's past, as heaven knows it is in both these murders, one spends a good deal of time waiting. Waiting for the autopsy report, the other forensic reports. Waiting, for quite a long time, for the DNA analysis if one has been ordered. Waiting for informants to turn up. Waiting for an inspiration. As I've said before, except for the rare occasions when police work is all too exciting, it's dull, Dorothy. It requires patience and perseverance."

"Well, patience may be a virtue," I retorted, "but it has never been one of mine. I want to do things now."

"Tomorrow," he said gently. "It's not so long. Tomorrow we'll talk to the doctor, and perhaps we can begin to make some progress."

Time does pass, of course, no matter how tedious the waiting. The pot does boil, no matter how assiduously it is watched. We got through the day, eventually. We spent the afternoon idly wandering around Madison, popping into antique and junk stores and looking at bits of history. We stopped at the historical society museum, bought a couple of books about Madison, and whiled away the evening reading them. Friday morning we packed up and took ourselves over to the Foleys' house.

Peggy welcomed us, settled us in our luxury suite in the guest cottage, and sat us down for lunch, chatting pleasantly. It wasn't until after we'd finished our lunch and were drinking excellent coffee ("The real stuff, since Doc isn't here") that she stopped talking about nothing and put down her coffee cup. "All right," she said quietly. "What are you really doing in Hillsburg?"

FIFTEEN

I LET OUT a long sigh. "Peggy, I'm so glad you asked. We're both dying to tell you all about it."

"It's about Kevin, isn't it?"

I think I gasped. "How did you know?"

"This is a small town, Dorothy. You've been talking to a lot of people. I hear Holy Bob tried to convert you from your sinful ways."

I shuddered at the memory. "That man is a menace. I'm afraid I don't have much use for that particular brand of religion."

Peggy snorted. "Religion my hind foot! Commerce is what it is. Did you see the car he drives?"

"No, but I can imagine. Cadillac?"

"Lincoln. Huge. Looks like a hearse. And his congregation's way too poor to keep him in that kind of luxury. But never mind him. Why are you asking questions about Kevin?"

Alan and I looked at each other. Alan rolled his eyes, and I groaned. "Oh, Lord, and we thought we were being subtle about it. We could be in real trouble if people are beginning to speculate. You see, we think Kevin was murdered."

Peggy took that, and the lengthy explanation that followed, in stride. I suppose a doctor's wife must hear a lot of peculiar things. "I thought it must be something like that," she said when I'd finished. "I know your reputation, you see. But it just isn't possible, is it? I mean, if Doc says he died of pneumonia, he died of pneumonia."

"I know. That's why I want to talk to Doc about it. Because, Peggy, there just isn't much doubt about it. We can't prove it yet, but we're reasonably certain in our own minds. Maybe there are ways to cause pneumonia?"

Peggy shrugged. "Stranger things have happened, I suppose. Though why anyone would want to get Kevin out of the way—Kevin, of all people!"

"I know," I said again. "That's what we thought at first. And the problem is—well, it sounds melodramatic, but one of the people we've talked to is probably...the one."

"Mmm. More coffee?"

We declined, and sat for a moment in worried silence. Then Peggy sat up straighter. If we'd been in a comic strip, a lightbulb would have appeared above her head.

"I've got it," she said triumphantly. "You're writing a book."

"Excuse me?"

"You're doing research. For a book about—about health patterns of the elderly. Or, no. The relationships between geriatric illness and social interactions."

"Why?"

She shrugged. "Kevin was an academic. This is a college town. Nobody'll ask why. People around here go and write fool books every day. Maybe you're doing some kind of postgraduate work in England. And you haven't told anybody what you're doing because...I know, because you didn't want their responses to be conditioned by the fact that they might be used in a book.''

I began to laugh. I couldn't help it. Alan laughed with me, and we giggled and snorted until tears came to our eyes and we had to hit each other on the back. At one point I was sure I was going to get the hiccups. Peggy waited, bewildered, until we had wiped our eyes and she had administered restorative glasses of water.

"All right," she said patiently. "What did I say?"

"I don't think," I gasped, still not fully in control of myself, "it was really what you said. We're a little tired and strung out, and it doesn't take much. The fact is, I told the police chief yesterday that I was writing a book. My version wasn't nearly as good as yours, though."

"Ah, well, you've left academic life and no longer imbibe academic jargon with your morning coffee. In this town it's in the air we breathe. So what's your version?"

"Just a biography. Nothing original at all."

"What a shame. Well, I suppose we'll have to stick with it, since you've already told one lie to the police. Changing to an entirely different one would complicate things. Okay, so we've dealt with *that* problem. I'll start spreading the word this afternoon when I go to the supermarket, and it'll be around in a day or two. Not, of course, that I believe for a moment that there's a problem anyway. It is simply not on the cards that Kevin was murdered."

"I think you're mistaken about that, Mrs. Foley."

Alan's voice was calm, reasonable.

"I'm Peggy. Okay, so you've both said you're convinced, and aside from that last little outburst, neither of you shows signs of certifiable insanity. What makes you believe such an unbelievable proposition?"

He methodically listed our reasons. The accidents. Kevin's talk with Father Kennedy. The circumstances of Jerry's death. "Too many coincidences," he concluded. "A policeman doesn't like coincidences."

"Mmm," said Peggy again, but it was a different kind of sound now. More like conditional agreement.

"Of course," Alan added, "we could do with something provable."

"What about Darryl Lacey? Can't he help? He talks with a real country twang, I know, but he's sharp."

Alan and I sighed in unison. "It isn't that we don't think he's a good cop," I explained. "It's just that he could be a suspect. I hadn't told you about it yet, but Kevin made a list, you see." I recited it.

"Aha! And he put 'doctor' on there, too. So what are you doing talking to me?"

I turned a little red, I think, but Alan's aplomb was equal to the situation.

"We have eliminated your husband on the grounds that (a) he was not in town when Kevin contracted his illness, and (b) he is not the sort of person who could ever kill anyone. I admit that the latter would not stand up in court, but as my dear wife insists that she would sooner suspect me than him, and as I trust her judgment..." He made a charming, deprecating gesture and grinned, and after a moment Peggy grinned back.

"Okay. But Darryl—I think you're all wet, suspecting him. Dorothy, we've both known him since he was a kid!"

"I know!" I ran my hands through my hair. "I don't want to suspect him! And it would be much easier if we could clear him for certain and start working together. But that's not as easy as it sounds. I'm getting very frustrated about all this, though Alan says we're making progress.''

"You're just too close to it, is all. Listen, Dorothy, you've written long letters to us, all about the stuff you've gotten involved in over in England, and I can read between the lines as well as anyone. There you could be objective. You were an observer. Oh, I know you've decided to live there and all, but—well, I hate to say it, but you don't quite belong there the way you do here. Hillsburg's your hometown, and your emotions are getting in the way.''

Alan had said much the same thing, hadn't he? The trouble was, I was beginning to feel I didn't belong anywhere, but I was going to have to take Alan's advice—ignore my feelings and get on with the job.

"You'll work it out," Peggy was saying. "The game tomorrow will get your adrenaline going and use up a lot of emotional energy, and you'll start looking at things with your usual jaundiced eye again.''

"Well, I must say! Jaundiced eye, indeed!''

"Your keen understanding of human nature, then, if you prefer it prettied up." She stood. "Now, if I don't get to the grocery, we'll have no dinner, and no tailgate party tomorrow. You want to come with me, or relax?''

"We'll come with you," Alan said promptly, to my surprise. "I've never been in an American supermarket, and I'd like to see one.''

He was a bit disappointed, I think. The local supermarket chain has very nice stores, but they're almost exactly like the big Tesco just outside Sherebury. I got lost once or twice in the aisles; they'd moved some of the departments since I'd been there last. When we got back we helped Peggy put things away, and then we repaired to our guest cottage, where I tried to explain

American football to Alan so he wouldn't feel left out the next day. We ended up collapsing on the bed in another bout of helpless laughter, and the sequel was very pleasant indeed.

We woke well before dinnertime. I felt refreshed and almost back in my right mind. "Alan, where's the notebook? I think we need to bring it up-to-date so we'll know what to ask Doc."

We hadn't made any entries for quite a few days now. I looked it over rather sadly. "Alan, I feel awful, writing down all this stuff about Jerry. Poor man! I think we should tear out everything about him."

Alan nodded sympathetically. "He's certainly out of the picture now, as a suspect. But we'll leave these entries. Who knows, they may help one day to identify his killer. Now look, we haven't filled in some of the interview sections."

We added a few comments about the lawyer, Ms. Carmichael ("closemouthed, cagey about Kevin's money") and the niece, Mrs. Harrison ("needs money, bitter about Kevin's will, bitter about life in general"). Mrs. Schneider got a note about her involvement in the Madison Tour of Homes.

"Not that that has anything to do with anything. In fact, nothing seems to have to do with anything. Are you *sure* we're not spinning our wheels?"

"We're gathering data," said Alan, unperturbed. "Something like ninety-seven percent of all data collected for police reports is irrelevant."

Somehow that didn't make me feel one bit better.

"And we have a whole section we can fill in here," he pointed out. "'What happened to make Kevin suspicious?' We have the answer to that now."

I nodded. "The accidents. Let's see, the car, the tricycle. His ankle. Was there anything else?"

"The telephone failures and the fire."

"Oh, yes." I wrote down the details. "Alan, we have to have dates for all this if we're to make any sort of pattern."

"We do, and how we're to get them without help from the police—"

I had no answer for that. We went back to the main house for dinner.

It was Doc, of all people, who threw the small bombshell. He came home somewhat late, tired and as nearly cross as I've ever seen him.

"That idiot of a Boland!" he fulminated as he collapsed into his special chair. Peggy handed him a glass of lemonade—he'd long ago forbidden himself any alcohol other than a little wine with dinner—and made soothing noises. "Yes, Peg, but you don't know what he's done!"

"Then tell us, and get it off your chest. Can I get you another drink, you two?"

"No, we're fine. What on earth's happened, Doc?"

"He's flown the coop, that's what! Just left town, and with sick patients needing him. I had to fit some of them in this afternoon, and I may not make it to the game tomorrow, either. The nincompoop!"

My mouth dropped open. I looked at Alan. He cleared his throat and asked the question.

"How very curious! Did Dr. Boland tell anyone why he was leaving, or where he was going?"

"Not a word to anybody, not even his office staff."

"What about his wife?"

"Doesn't have one. Divorced, I think."

"So how do you know..." I began slowly. "I mean,

something might have happened to him. An accident, or he could be ill, or..." Thoughts of Jerry rose in my mind. I took a rather large sip of my drink.

"We figured it was something like that," said Doc. "He's got a housekeeper—maid—cleaning lady—don't know what to call her. Anyway, she comes in every day to clean and do his laundry and cook his dinner and whatever, and she's got a key. So Boland's secretary called her, and she went over there." Doc gulped down half his lemonade and made a face. "I could sure use something stronger. Wish I weren't such a good candidate for a heart attack.

"So the woman checked Boland's clothes. They're almost all gone, and so is all his luggage and his car. The Lord only knows why, but it looks as if he's just flat out left home!"

"Oh, I think somebody besides the Lord might have an idea," said Peggy, meaningfully.

"What? What d'you mean?"

"I think you'd better tell him, Dorothy."

I took a deep breath. "It's a long story," I warned, and launched into it.

"So you see," I finished, "it does look more than a little suspicious that Dr. Boland has disappeared this way. Though why he'd want to kill either Kevin or poor Jerry..."

I let the thought trail off. There was a little silence, and then Doc held up his glass. "Peggy, take this damn stuff away and bring me some scotch!"

SIXTEEN

WE THRASHED IT OUT over dinner.

"He died of pneumonia!" Doc said over and over. "There's no way Jim could have killed him."

He was "Boland," I noticed, when Doc was mad at him; "Jim" when he was being defended. I smiled a little grimly. I wasn't so sure defense was appropriate.

"Potassium injected into the IV line," I suggested tentatively. "That would have been easy for Dr. Boland to do."

"So you know about that little trick, do you?" Doc growled. "That case up in Vigo County where the nurse killed all those people, that what you're thinking about? Well, you can stop thinking about it. Even if we hadn't taken a routine K-level—a potassium check—every so often, which we did, I ordered a private nurse for Kevin the last couple of days. He was never alone. Nobody put anything in his IV that wasn't supposed to be there. I was with him myself the last couple of hours." He glared at us, in response to a criticism nobody was making. "All right, there was nothing I could do, and I knew it, and I should have been tending to my business, but he'd been a friend for a long time! He died absolutely peacefully, and typically for pneumonia. His breaths were spaced farther and farther apart, and finally—the next one just didn't come." He lifted his glass of wine, took a sip, and applied himself to cutting his chicken into little pieces, which he didn't eat.

"Forgive me for suggesting it," said Alan, "but could Dr. Boland have caused Kevin's pneumonia in some way? I'm quite ignorant about medical matters, but if he had another patient with pneumonia, could he perhaps have prepared a culture of some sort…?" He trailed off at the look on Doc's face.

"Aside from the fact that it would be damn hard to do, there's the fact that Jim had never met Kevin until shortly before he was admitted to the hospital. How do you think he'd have gotten a virus into him? And why?"

That, really, was the pivotal question. Why would Dr. Boland want Kevin, a man he didn't know, dead? I ate my meal in silence, wild thoughts chasing each other around my head. Boland was a doctor. Kevin, in his younger days, had developed antibiotics. What if one of them had gone wrong somehow and killed one of Boland's patients? But no, that was absurd. Boland was the younger man by forty or fifty years. By the time he had entered practice, Kevin's discoveries had long since been replaced by more modern drugs.

Well, then, maybe Kevin knew something about Boland, something to his discredit.

"Where did Dr. Boland go to school?" I asked abruptly, interrupting an argument about medical ethics. "Did he do his pre-med at Randolph?"

"Not Randolph," said Doc patiently, "but I have no idea where. He's from the South somewhere. Got his M.D. at—I can't remember, but one of the southern schools. Does it matter?"

"I thought he might have known Kevin years ago."

"Still harping on the idea he might have killed him, are you? I tell you it's impossible."

"Okay. It's impossible. But then why did he sneak out of town?"

There was plenty of speculation about that. "Trouble over a woman" was Peggy's idea. "I've never liked him. He's a cold fish, the kind who'd use a woman and then throw her away."

"Perhaps he was involved in something illegal," said Alan, thinking like the policeman he was. "The drugs trade would seem the most likely possibility."

"I'm convinced," I said stubbornly, "that Dr. Boland has a guilty secret of some kind. Kevin found out about it and threatened to tell. And no, I have no idea how Kevin was killed, but I'll bet Dr. Boland was in it up to his neck."

"Has anybody called the police?" Peggy asked.

"I did," said Doc, "once I realized he was gone. They won't do anything, just keep on saying it isn't illegal to leave home voluntarily."

"Unless you're running away from something," I said darkly.

"Well, legal or not, it's still damned irresponsible! If they find out he's left a lot of unpaid bills behind him, I suppose his creditors will be after him, but for now he's free as a bird."

We talked about it all evening, but nobody had any brilliant ideas. Alan and I took the discussion to bed with us.

"I want to find out about his past," I said as we settled down to sleep. "That's one thing that needn't involve Darryl, thank goodness."

"How do you work that out?" asked Alan, yawning.

"His diplomas will be in his office. I know enough about academia to know how to trace records back. I still know a lot of people in Randolph's registrar's office.

By tomorrow afternoon I'll know all about Dr. James Boland's background, academically, at least.''

"Tomorrow," said Alan with sleepy brevity, "is Saturday.''

"The registrar's office is open Saturday morning—"

"And we are booked to attend a football game.''

"Oh. I forgot.'' I sighed. "I suppose we have to go. But we could go to his office, first thing in the morning, and look up the diplomas.''

I paused for Alan's reaction to that plan. My answer was a gentle snore.

I HAD MANAGED, after several years away from it, to forget the bedlam that prevailed in Hillsburg on a football Saturday. There was no question of a visit, however brief, to Dr. Boland's office. The traffic was moving like a nest of torpid snakes. I did think, when I first woke up, of asking Doc to check out the diplomas, but he had already left when Alan and I arrived at the house for breakfast.

"Hoping to get Jim's patients out of the way before the game," said Peggy. She slammed the refrigerator door with a violence that jiggled the dishes on the table. "Really, that man! The first Saturday Doc's taken off in a month, and Boland has to go and spoil it!''

"Maybe nobody's very sick, and Doc will make it to the stadium after all,'' I said hopefully. I no longer had the slightest interest in the game, but I had worked out several new questions for Doc. "Now, what can I do to help?''

After a hurried breakfast we began work on a picnic lunch. Baked chicken—"We used to fry it, but Doc's cholesterol is just barely under control, and I'm trying to bring it down"—salads, baked beans, vegetables and salsa for finger food, fruit, rolls, and a marvelous, rich-looking dessert. "Doc loves chocolate, and this one's low-fat—believe it or not. Okay, that's it, I think, except for the drinks, and they're in the cooler in the van. Let's pack it up and move it out."

I looked at my watch. "Peggy, it's ten o'clock! Surely we don't need to start this early. It isn't more than fifteen minutes to the stadium. Wouldn't it be simpler just to eat an early lunch here and drive over afterward?"

She grinned. "You *have* become Anglicized! Have you forgotten how long it takes to get to campus on a football day? Or what the parking lot is like?"

I had indeed forgotten. I was quickly reminded. It was pandemonium, but we were early enough to claim our small piece of turf.

"What," Alan asked mildly, "are we to do for the next three hours? The game does not, I believe, begin until one-thirty."

"First of all," I said, taking his arm, "you buy a mum corsage for me and a pennant for yourself and a program for both of us."

He had to be told about the traditional game souvenirs, but once he caught on, he gallantly insisted on buying one of the big corsages for Peggy, too. I, of course, purchased a black and orange hat, the kind sailors wear, featuring a large embroidered tiger. Then we worked our way through the program. Everything had to be explained to Alan.

"It sounds," he said finally, "as though matters proceed rather slowly in this game."

I turned to Peggy. "Have you ever, on your trips to England, watched a cricket match? They go on for days sometimes."

For once, Alan was silenced.

We took a walk before lunch. It was a beautiful day, sunny and crisp, perfect weather for football or a stroll, and Alan hadn't seen this part of the campus.

"This end hasn't changed quite as much as where we were the other day. There's the field house, where they used to have the basketball games before they built the new sports arena. Then this whole area here is the engineering part of campus." I pointed at buildings in turn, reciting, "Mechanical, chemical, electrical, civil. There are some more tigers, see? On that gate."

"I'm not sure I understand the purpose of the gate. There is no wall or fence."

"No purpose at all. It's a memorial to someone or other whose heirs thought it looked fancy. Now, this is the Biological Sciences Building."

Alan squeezed my hand. "Where Frank used to teach."

"And Kevin."

We said nothing more on our way back to the stadium.

We didn't wait lunch for Doc. He arrived, somewhat breathless and red-faced, just as we were thinking about dessert.

"Decided it was easier to leave the car where it was and walk over," he explained. "Managed to get rid of the last patient half an hour ago. Kid with measles. They're bad this year; I just hope he didn't give them to everybody else in the office. Oh, and Dorothy, I took a look at Jim's diplomas for you, since you were so het up about his background. He got his B.S. at the University of Virginia and his M.D. at Johns Hopkins. Don't know where he interned."

He gave his attention to his belated meal while I thought about that. Johns Hopkins was a very fine med-

ical school with a very fine reputation. What was one of
their graduates doing in a little backwater like Hillsburg?

I worried at the idea like a dog with a bone, so preoccupied that I don't remember finding our seats in the
stadium. The band played, the game began, the crowd
grew boisterous. It was only background noise.

Why had he come here? I loved Hillsburg myself, but
it was not an obviously attractive place to live, not for
a stranger. The standard of living was nothing like as
high as in bigger cities. Salaries were moderate. The
climate was fairly pleasant, but distinctly chilly for
someone from the South.

Did Boland have such a poor academic record that he
had to take what he could get? Did Johns Hopkins let
students with poor records graduate? And if so, why
would Doc turn patients over to him, even occasionally?
Or would Doc check the academic record? Wouldn't he
just go by the kind of doctor Boland seemed to be?

The crowd stood up and roared, and I stood and roared
with them, waving my hat. "Wow! Look at him go!
Touchdown!"

The crowd quieted. Peggy looked at me and touched
her head meaningfully. "Yeah. Touchdown. Pity it was
Notre Dame's. Either pay attention or keep your mouth
shut, or you'll get lynched. And put your hat on."

"Oh." I sat back down and lost myself in thought
again.

Maybe Boland had gotten into some kind of trouble
while he was in medical school. Something that
wouldn't get into his record, but would make it a good
idea for him to seek work far afield. Or maybe it had
been during his internship. Interns made a lot of mistakes, working on too little sleep and too much caffeine.
Or other drugs. At least, that used to be the case. I'd

read that conditions had improved somewhat in recent years. When would Boland have been an intern, though? Quite a while ago. Let's see. Suppose he was forty-five. He'd looked about that. Twenty-one when he finished his pre-med, twenty-five when he got his M.D. Twenty years ago, then, he'd been an intern. At least twenty years. He could well be older than forty-five.

The crowd groaned. At least those around me did. I looked up and perceived that the ball soaring past some-one's outstretched hands was a pass that our side had been meant to catch, and hadn't.

"Doc!" I had to shout; he was three seats away. "Doc, when did Dr. Boland finish his internship?"

"Idiot! Butterfingers! What did you say, Dorothy?"

I repeated the question.

"How should I know?"

"Well, I meant, when did he come to Hillsburg? I never heard of him before, but then I never really knew any doctor but you."

"Oh, he's after your time. Only been here two or three—did you see that? Peg, did you see that? Snatched it away just in the nick of—RUN, you nincompoop!"

The crowd surged to its feet again. The runner, who had apparently gotten the ball from the hands of the enemy, was tackled shortly before he reached the goal line—ours, this time, I was pretty sure. Alan looked at me with raised eyebrows.

"First down. That means Randolph has four tries to make another ten yards. And they're only a little farther than that from the goal line, so if they don't quite make it, they'll probably try for a field goal on the fourth."

"I see." He didn't sound sure. I dutifully watched the next play, a depressing one. Randolph was pushed back a good five yards.

"I thought they were moving in that direction." Alan pointed to our goal.

"They're trying to. That Notre Dame line has some awfully big guys."

The next two plays accomplished nothing. Randolph kicked and didn't make it. I lost interest again.

So Boland had been in town only a couple of years. That made the matter much more interesting. There were a lot of years of practice to account for in there, a lot of years when something disastrous could have happened. Whatever it was, it must have been a lulu, to make a man leave an established practice and come to a little town in southern Indiana.

By halftime the score was fifteen to nothing, the crowd was despondent, and I had considered every possible iniquity from drug dealing to murder. I tried to ask Doc a couple of questions, but he was too irate over the sins of the Randolph coach to pay much attention, and the band was playing too loudly for us to hear each other, anyway.

I used to enjoy the halftime shows, but either the performance standard had slipped, or I was too preoccupied. Certainly the seat had become very hard. I got up in the middle of a rousing jazz number and shouted in Alan's ear. "I'm getting stiff. I'm going for a walk."

"Shall I come with you?"

"Not unless you want to."

"Sure?"

"Sure."

"I'll stay, then. I'm rather enjoying the show."

I wasn't sure if he meant the game, or the band, or the crowd, or the whole experience, but it didn't matter, so long as he was having a good time. I squeezed past a long row of fans and made my way to the vast concourse under the stadium seats.

It was crowded with people seeking food or drink or the rest rooms. I found a ladies' room, made a prudent stop, and then resumed pacing. What was Boland's guilty secret? Why had he left town? Where was he?

"Why, Dorothy Martin, as I live and breathe!"

It took me a moment to identify the man who was blocking my way and beaming. Bald as an egg and running to fat, he looked vaguely familiar....

"Bet you don't recognize me! I've changed a little, I guess, but you haven't. Still the same Polka Dot."

Now I knew. "Zeke Jasinski! No, I hadn't forgotten, my brain just doesn't work as fast as it used to. You're looking fine!"

"Now, don't try to butter me up. I'm old and bald, and too fat to polka much anymore."

"I'll bet you still dance at Polish weddings! We used to be pretty good, didn't we?"

"That we did. It was my luck your husband didn't like to dance any more than my wife did."

"Yes, well..." They were both gone now. It was a subject to avoid. "What are you doing here? I thought you moved away."

"And so did you. Yeah, I live in Florida now. But I still get season tickets every year. Once a Randolph fan, always a Randolph fan, you know. Not sure why I keep coming, as lousy as the team's been these past few years, but they've got to get better eventually, don't they?"

"I hope so. That first half was pretty dismal."

An air horn shrieked, cutting through the noise in the concourse.

"Woops! Second half's starting, gotta go. You going anyplace afterward?"

"I'm with some people; I'm not sure."

"Well, then—great to see you!"

He vanished in the great swirl of people heading for the gangways. Thank goodness he hadn't tried to exchange addresses and insincere promises to stay in touch. I'd enjoyed the Polish weddings Frank and I had attended with the Jasinskis and the boisterous polkas I'd danced with Zeke, but I had no desire to renew our acquaintance.

I shouldn't, I mused as I struggled toward my seat, have been surprised to see him there. Even when one's life changes drastically, when one loses a spouse, or moves far away from home, one tends to keep to the old patterns as much as possible. The habits of a lifetime don't change easily, and there is vast comfort in the familiar. Even after Frank died and I moved to England, I went on reading mysteries, and cooking, and looking after the cats, and going to church, and doing crossword puzzles—the things I'd enjoyed for a lifetime.

An idea began to glimmer. By the time I reached my row, it was shining brightly.

"Doc," I said, stopping in front of him on my way to my seat, "what did Dr. Boland enjoy doing? What were his hobbies?"

Doc looked up from the program he was scanning in an attempt to find some ray of hope in the lineup. "Hobbies? Don't know. He didn't like sports, I know that. Never went to a football game in his life."

"Opera, Doc," put in Peggy. "Good heavens, don't you remember the time he dragged us to that performance of some modern thing? We were bored to tears, but he loved it. Oh, look, here they come."

The crowd on our side of the stands loyally cheered our outmatched team as they took the field. I cheered right along with them. I'd struck gold.

SEVENTEEN

SUNDAY MORNING, as soon as Alan and I got back from church, I asked Peggy about her plans for the day.

"No plans. I'm going to lie around the house and do as close to nothing as I can manage. Meals of leftovers whenever anyone wants to raid the refrigerator. Why, did you have something in mind?"

"I thought Alan and I might drive up to Bloomington. It's a beautiful day and I'd like him to see the IU campus. IU is Indiana University, Alan. But, Peggy, I'm embarrassed about treating your house like a hotel. I don't suppose you and Doc would like to come with us?"

"Thanks, but no thanks. I'm pooped, and Doc is still crabby about the game. Go and enjoy yourselves, and don't come back till you feel like it. You've got the key."

It was a pretty drive. I took the back roads through the rolling southern Indiana hills I love so much. We saw tobacco hung up to dry in barns; I pointed it out to Alan.

"I had no idea it grew this far north," he commented.

"This part of Indiana's pretty southern in many ways. I feel sorry for the Indiana tobacco farmers, though. They didn't make a lot of money at the best of times, and with the demand for tobacco falling off, the little guys are the first to be hurt. The stuff's a scourge, of course, but it seems like someone ought to think of some way to help the farmers whose livelihood depends on it.''

Alan sighed. He still missed the pipe he'd given up only a few months before. ''It would be a boon, not only to them, but to mankind, if they could render the wretched stuff harmless.''

I smiled. ''I think it was one of Elizabeth Peters's characters who decided that heaven was a place where you could smoke and not get lung cancer.''

''Or emphysema, or congestive heart failure, or any of the other ills that tobacco-poisoned flesh is heir to. Dorothy, what are you up to?''

I guess I jumped at that; the car swerved a little on the steep hill. I slowed and brought it back under control.

''What do you mean, up to?''

''Yesterday you were panting to follow the trail of the bolted Dr. Boland. You resented every moment you had to spend at that remarkable exercise in sport. Today you decide to leave town on an ostensible pleasure jaunt. I agree the drive is pleasant, but you are up to something.''

''You know me too well, that's the trouble. All right, if you must know, I discovered yesterday a trail I could follow, and I'm following it.''

''And what sort of trail is that?''

''I'm not going to tell you until it works. If it does. Look at the corn shocks in that field! You sure don't see those much anymore.''

Alan smiled appreciatively, though I wasn't certain whether it was at the cornfield or at my attempt at diversion.

We arrived in Bloomington just before noon and, after a quick lunch, drove to campus. ''There's no point trying to drive around the university, even on a Sunday," I told Alan. "Too crowded. We'll just go straight to the MAC and see if we can park on the street near there."

"What's the MAC?"

"The Musical Arts Center. A big opera house founded, in part, by Hoagie Carmichael."

I looked at him, checking for recognition. He smiled in delighted surprise. "'Stardust'? 'Up a Lazy River'? 'Old Man Moon'?"

"That's the guy. I didn't know you liked that kind of music."

"I grew up on it. Especially 'Stardust.' I fell in love once to 'Stardust.' The romance didn't last long, but my love for the music did. What did Hoagie Carmichael have to do with the University of Indiana?"

"Indiana University. He's one of their most famous sons. He was a student here. Not a music student; he never learned to read music. I think he studied law or something. But he's supposed to have written 'Stardust' in the Book Nook, a student hangout, and his name is forever associated with this campus. That's why he gave a lot of money to help build the MAC. His funeral was even held in the lobby."

We parked easily. "Good. There isn't a performance this afternoon."

"But what an enormous building! Surely a university performance couldn't draw a big enough audience to fill a place this size."

"We're not talking amateur hour here," I said patiently. "The Indiana University Opera Theatre is famous. Eileen Farrell used to teach here, you know, and the students are so good the Met holds auditions for new talent, right here on campus, every year."

"Good heavens." We had gotten out of the car and

wandered up to the front of the building. The place was shut up tight, but there were posters listing the operas scheduled for the season. Alan read them off. "*The Rake's Progress. Rigoletto. L'Elisir d'amore. The Magic Flute. Tosca.* That's a demanding season."

"*The Rake's Progress.* Excellent! And it opens on Thursday. We're going to that performance, Alan."

"Stravinsky? Now, Dorothy, I'm not sure I—"

"Stravinsky's not all that far out, and I've never seen this particular work. We're going."

Neither of us is given, usually, to unilateral decisions. We tend to defer to the other's wishes. Alan opened his mouth and looked at me, and then the light dawned.

"The trail."

I grinned. "I hope. I found out yesterday that Dr. Boland's an opera lover. He especially likes modern stuff. IU Opera is not only terrific, it's close to Hillsburg. I'll bet he buys season tickets every year."

"But, according to your theory, the man's on the run. Surely he won't take time to go to the opera!"

"Maybe not. But I'm betting he will. He'll think himself perfectly safe in a big, festive crowd. It's the gala opening, after all." I expounded my theory that people don't change old habits. "It's worth a try, anyway."

"It would be very much simpler to let the police track him down."

"Yes, but we can't ask them to. We can't tell them what we know about Boland."

"In fact, my dear, though you'll loathe my saying so, we don't *know* anything at all."

"We know Boland is an opera freak," I retorted. "And I intend to be here Thursday night, looking for him."

Alan shrugged and capitulated. "*If* we can get tickets."

That, I admitted, might require some doing. The season opener would have been sold out for weeks. As we strolled over the beautiful campus with its graceful stone buildings ("Indiana limestone. One of the best building stones in the world!" I bragged), I thought about ways and means, and Monday morning, back in our hotel again, I started making phone calls.

I was on the phone all morning, and by noon I had tracked down only one ticket, from a long-ago friend who was down with the flu and only too glad to get her money back. "If it were Puccini I'd have gone anyway, if I were dying. But Stravinsky..."

Alan was not devastated at the thought that he might miss the opera. "Don't worry, love. I can lurk about outside if the evening's fine, or in the lobby."

"I'll keep trying, but—"

"Don't worry," he repeated. "I didn't bring my dress suit, in any case."

"Oh, love, almost none of the men wear black tie anymore, even for the opening. It's a great pity, I think, but I didn't bring anything fancy, either, so it's just as well."

"You'll look lovely in anything you wear. Now, what's next on the agenda?"

"I want to look up Boland's academic record. Let's go over to the registrar's office and see if anybody I know still works there."

"Why don't you go? I'd only be a nuisance, and I've hatched a few ideas of my own."

"Are you going to tell?"

"No. If you're entitled to secrets, so am I. I will say only that I am beginning to work out the processes for investigation without benefit of authority. It isn't as easy as one might think. I have a new respect for your successes over the years, my dear.''

I grinned as he left. He was beginning to enjoy this.

I detoured, on my way to the university, to the building where Boland and Doc Foley had their offices. I wanted to see the dates on Boland's diplomas. I had an elaborate story prepared for his secretary, but as it happened, she was not in the office. The lights were on, the door was unlocked, and the phone was ringing. I assumed she had left for the usual reason and slipped cautiously into the back premises, finding Boland's private office easily. It was as I had thought. Dr. Boland had finished medical school over twenty years ago.

I got out with no trouble and went over to the registrar's office, where I thought at first I was going to have much less luck. The registrar himself, an old friend, had retired. His replacement was one of those shiny MBA types with the bionic personality. The title on his door was Director of Student Services. He was delighted to meet me. What a shame Mr. Resnick was no longer with the university. He would be sure to pass along my greetings the next time they got together. Nice to meet you, Mrs. Morton. His broad smile didn't reach beyond his mouth, and his handclasp was painful.

I certainly couldn't ask him to do a little unauthorized snooping.

I wandered, a trifle disconsolate, through the halls. The layout was very different from the way I remembered it. Offices had been reconfigured, new partitions erected, signs moved. Nothing is static in a university, but the changes made me feel lost and forlorn and very much a back number.

"May I help you?" The voice was young and bright

and chirpy. In my present mood, I found it offensively condescending.

"I very much doubt it," I snapped. "I was looking for someone I used to know, but it isn't important."

"I still have trouble finding people myself." The owner of the voice, an attractive girl—woman, I suppose—who couldn't have been more than twenty, giggled. "They moved everybody at the beginning of the semester when they changed everything around. Who were you trying to find?"

The child was trying to help. I struggled to control my surliness. "Sharon Clark. She used to be—"

"Oh, sure! This place would fall down without her. She's got a new office, around the corner down there. First door on the right." She smiled and sped on her way before I could thank her and apologize for being rude.

The first door on the right around the corner opened on a small office, nice and private. Sharon was sitting at her desk, her attention on a computer screen, but she looked up when I appeared in the doorway.

"Well, good grief, you never know who's going to turn up! Dorothy, how *are* you? And what are you doing back in town, and how long are you going to stay, and when can you go to lunch with me?"

I laughed and sat down. "I'm fine, and I don't know for sure how long I'll be here, and any time you like, and how are you?"

"Busy, busy. My new boss"—she looked up at the door and lowered her voice—"is something else."

"I saw him," I said dryly. "Looks like a cross between Donald Trump, Attila the Hun, and C-3PO."

"You got that right. In just about equal parts. So what

have you been doing? You haven't come back to stay, then?''

"No, I'm pretty well settled down in England. You knew I'd remarried?''

"I heard, and I was thrilled. Some people around here got bent out of shape, because they liked the professor so much, but I said good grief, she's got her life to live, Dr. Martin wouldn't have wanted her to go on being lonesome forever. What's he like?''

"You'll find out when we go to lunch. Are you free tomorrow?''

"You bet. Noon?''

"We'll pick you up. Now, Sharon, I have to admit I didn't stop by just for old times' sake. I have an ulterior motive.''

She grinned. "You want me to look somebody up for you.''

"If you can. I don't know if he ever took any courses here, so you might not have a record. Do you have access to the Continuing Ed side of things?''

"Not officially, but I can get in if I have to.''

A little adventure a while back had taught me a thing or two about computers and those who operate them. "I'll just bet you can!''

She turned to her keyboard. "I don't suppose you have a social security number?''

"No, just a name. James F. Boland.'' I spelled the last name. She typed it in, and I waited, actually holding my breath.

"Ah, you're in luck! A doctor, would he be? Medical, I mean?''

"Yes. You've found him?''

"There isn't much. He took a couple of CE courses

a year, just keeping up with new developments, I expect. And he did take one credit course.''

That surprised me. "Really? What? Chemistry? Biology?''

"Music. A graduate course in opera history.''

Of course. His passion. I smiled to myself. He was probably a royal pain in the neck in the class, knowing more than any of the other students and very possibly more than the teacher. But I was very glad he'd taken the class, all the same. "A graduate course. So he would have had to submit his transcripts from his other education.''

"Yes. Of course we wouldn't have those. We don't keep any paper records centrally anymore. They'd be in the music department.''

I moistened my lips. "And I don't suppose you'd have any reason to look at them?''

She didn't even hesitate. "We do need, every so often, to check and make sure records are complete. The new director is very particular about complete records.'' With a perfectly straight face, she picked up the phone. "Hello, Donna? This is Sharon. Hi. Listen, I'm going over some stuff, and I need to check some transcripts. Could you pull some files for me?'' She was typing as she spoke, and I saw a list of names appear on her screen. "They're all graduate students. Gerald Bodine— okay, ready? Gerald Bodine, James Boland, Charles Hatcher, and Susan Miller. Do you want their ID numbers? No. Right. Okay, I'll send somebody over for them in—half an hour all right?''

She put the phone down. "I didn't want to make it obvious.''

"You're wonderful. I owe you one.''

"For what? If I should happen to have some students'

files on my desk when you come tomorrow to pick me up for lunch, there's nothing unusual about that, is there? And if I should happen to need to powder my nose, and you should happen to notice something in one of the files, well, neither of us can really be blamed for that, can we?''

"Of course not. Can you take an extra-long lunch tomorrow? And where's your favorite place?"

I left feeling jubilant enough to smile brilliantly at the boss robot on my way out.

EIGHTEEN

I GOT BACK TO the room before Alan and was just trying to decide whether to take a nap or study the case notebook when he came in.

"You look," I said, "exactly the way Emmy-cat did that time she caught that disgusting rat half her size. Triumphant and smug. What's up?"

"I have spent a most productive afternoon, my dear." He produced a paper bag of suspicious size and shape. "I looked more than slightly disreputable walking home with this. There is really no way to carry a bottle that does not make it look like a bottle. I did, however, refrain from drinking out of it until I returned. I felt a small celebration might be in order."

"Well, you know I'm always ready for a celebration, especially when it involves Jack Daniel's." Alan poured us each a small tot and we sat down around the small table. I raised my glass. "Very well, what are we celebrating?"

"The acquisition of knowledge." He clicked my glass.

"Oh, you can be infuriating when you want to be!"

He smiled his catlike smile again. "Can I, my dear? That's very gratifying."

"Okay, but I'm not going to tell you a thing until you tell me. As," I added, "you are pining to do."

"I am. It is, however, pleasant to be persuaded." He took another sip from his glass and set it down. "I spent the time in your newspaper office."

I waited.

"I find the local newspaper to be an interesting phenomenon. We do not, of course, have them in England. Aside from the odd local weekly—odd in both senses— we rely on the large national papers for our edification."

"Yes, dear, I do know. I've lived there for some time, you may remember."

"Indeed. I mention it only because I find it a pity that we have never adopted the notion of a daily local journal. Although the coverage of national news is somewhat sketchy and the world outside the United States appears not to exist for the editors of the *Hillsburg Herald,* it nevertheless proved to be a mine of information."

"About—?"

"About the accidents." He grew more serious. "You remember that we wished to know more about the accidents that befell Kevin. Or, more strictly speaking, the various incidents."

He ticked them off. "The failure of the brakes on his automobile. The theft of his tricycle. The repeated failures of his telephone. The fire. His fall down the steps.

"The *Herald* prints, daily, a most useful report. I had noticed it whilst reading the copy this establishment kindly delivers to our door every morning. One can, by reading a good deal of very small type, learn about all the incidents requiring the attention of the police and/or fire departments on the previous day."

I raised my glass. "So you looked up the things that happened to Kevin. Well done! I hadn't thought of that."

His smug look intensified. He sipped his drink and

then pressed his fingertips together in the tent formation that usually means he's about to deliver a lecture. "When one is handicapped by the lack of access to official police reports, one must make do."

"You sound," I commented, "exactly like Bunter pontificating to Lord Peter."

He ignored me and continued. "Many of the incidents, of course, were not in the police-fire reports. In fact, I found only two there. The first, the brakes on the car, figured in a report of an abandoned vehicle. Apparently someone saw the car before it was towed away and reported it. And the tricycle was reported as stolen. That gave me dates for two incidents."

"What about the fire?"

"If you remember, Kevin's phone wasn't working then. Apparently he never reported it later, either. At any rate, there was no record. So I then proceeded," he went on, sounding for all the world like a police report himself, "to other sections of the newspaper."

"And?"

"And I discovered two items of considerable interest. The first was dated two days after Kevin's tricycle was stolen. It was a syndicated column by a humorist whose wit, I fear, I was unable to appreciate. He went on for some time about small household disasters that certainly didn't seem funny. However, he did mention a persistent telephone problem that no one could diagnose."

"Aha!"

"You understand my interest. In his account, it transpired that a squirrel had chewed through part of the telephone cable. One of the two wires was damaged. The problem was intermittent because the wire would maintain contact so long as the wind did not blow. When it did, the phone would not function. The damage couldn't easily be seen."

"You think a squirrel…?"

"Possibly. I am more inclined to think that someone saw that column, someone who had tried at least twice to cause Kevin's death. That someone got an idea."

"And frayed Kevin's telephone wire! Someplace where it couldn't be easily seen or repaired."

"Or, just possibly, a place where it *could* be easily repaired—just before Kevin phoned for repairs."

"Oh, that's brilliant, Alan! Diabolical, but brilliant. So not only would the repairmen be unable to find anything wrong, they'd begin to think Kevin was some sort of crank and be slower and slower to respond. AND they'd charge him an arm and a leg."

"Charge? For no work?"

"We have a weird phone system in this country. If you call the phone company and the problem is in their lines, they fix it for nothing. If it isn't, though, not only do they not fix it, they hit you with a hefty charge for a service call."

Alan shook his head sadly. "Someone is very clever, Dorothy. *But*—do you want to know what else I read in the newspaper?"

"I can't wait. So far, you've come up trumps every time."

"You'll not like this one so well, I fear, but I believe you'll agree it's interesting information. It was simply a very small news item on the business page, listing the names of area physicians who had attended a seminar on various rare diseases. One of those listed was Dr. Boland."

"Oh, I already knew he was conscientious about

keeping informed. Let me tell you what I found out to-day.''

''Wait, let me finish. The date of the seminar was the day Kevin's tricycle was stolen.''

''But—but—''

''Yes, indeed. Dr. Boland could not have been responsible for that incident. And if we assume it to have been one of a series…''

''But then *why* did he leave town?''

We were right back where we'd been three days before, with a fugitive and no explanation for his flight.

NINETEEN

I HAD TROUBLE SLEEPING that night. For once Alan's warm presence beside me offered little comfort. I punched my pillow into a more satisfactory shape, rolled over to my right side, and recited the multiplication table in my head.

My knee hurt, and my foot was trying to cramp. I rolled onto my stomach and tried reciting the Twenty-third Psalm.

Sleeping on my stomach was very bad for my back. I rolled onto my left side.

My nightgown was wound around my waist like a tourniquet. I heaved and tugged, hitting Alan with my elbow. He grunted once and continued snoring.

I was seized with the irrational resentment of the sleeper that possesses the sleepless. It was all very well for him, him in his comfortable oblivion. What did he care if I was awake and restless and miserable?

I sighed—loudly—and punched the pillow once more—hard.

No reaction.

You would *think*, with all the walking you've done in the past few days, that you'd be too tired for this, I told myself crossly. You would *think* you'd fall asleep as soon as your head hit the pillow. But no, all the exercise has done is make your knees ache more.

The pillow was still the wrong shape. Exasperated, I got up and went to the bathroom for a glass of tepid hotel water.

The fact was, of course, that my restlessness had nothing to do with the pillow, nothing to do with the hard mattress or the minor aches and pains that were always with me now. The trouble was in my mind. I was annoyed with myself, and no amount of tossing and turning and pillow-punching was going to help that.

It was all very well for Alan to say we were making progress, but it was all so *slow*. I wanted things to come to a head. I wanted something to *happen*. I wanted to find out something definitive, something that would get us somewhere. So far we'd uncovered absolutely nothing that would lead us to Kevin's killer. All we had done, Alan and I, was to place ourselves under police suspicion and restrict our ability to accomplish anything useful.

True, we were both convinced that Kevin had not died a natural death. And what good did that do? I thought bitterly. We couldn't prove anything about his death. We didn't *know* anything about Jerry's death, which was certainly related.

Or was it? I was at that dark stage of self-doubt that flourishes, rank and weedy, at midnight of a sleepless night. Maybe Darryl Lacey was right. Maybe Jerry had been killed in the aftermath of a drunken brawl. Maybe Kevin had been imagining things. Maybe Alan and I should go back home where people knew us and believed us.

That thought set me to pacing the floor. Home. I was home, wasn't I?

Not anymore, said the horrid little voice that loves to torment me from time to time. *This isn't home anymore. Do you even have a home anymore?*

The room was warm. Too warm. I opened the window, but no breath of air was stirring. Oh, wonderful. We were in for a spell of the kind of weather Hillsburg occasionally gets in October. Not Indian summer, with the pleasant warmth that implied, but stormy July, three months late. Hot, humid, unsettling.

Maybe if I went for a walk? There might be some air I could breathe outside, maybe a breeze that would blow the cobwebs out of my head.

I dressed as quietly as I could, put a note on my pillow in case Alan woke and worried—*not that he will,* the nasty inner voice sneered—and stole out of the room.

A little common sense began to assert itself once I was actually outside. The air, muggy and still, was really no more refreshing than inside the hotel. It was after midnight. Was this a stupid thing to do? I wouldn't hesitate to take a midnight stroll back at home—back in Sherebury, I firmly corrected myself. But this was America, with a crime rate, even in little Hillsburg, that would send Sherebury into shock.

Oh, for Pete's sake! I was in a bad mood, and it was making me silly. The campus was well lighted and well patrolled. The hour was not late, not for students. There would be people around, and none of them would be interested in a middle-aged lady—all right, verging on old—going about her business.

I crossed the street.

By night, the campus seemed far more familiar than by day. The basic layout was still the same, and darkness hid most of the recent changes. The lovely old oak and maple trees were in the same places, and so were the old buildings, empty now of the teeming energy that enlivened them during the day, slumbering in their creaky dustiness.

They were impervious to change, those ivied halls. The students might come and go, their dress changing over the generations, the forms of their rebellion. The faculty, more slowly, changed from wing collars to tweed jackets with leather patches to blue jeans and T-shirts, and they, too, rang new changes on the old academic ideals. All of them left their faint impressions on the fabric of the buildings: the worn stair treads, the floors scraped by hundreds of chairs. The bricks, though, the stone and glass and wood, these endured essentially changeless, except for the intangible atmosphere of learning, of academic endeavor, that had been absorbed over the years and would continue to linger and radiate until the buildings themselves were dust.

I rambled along my favorite paths, now and then encountering a couple locked in an embrace. None of them noticed me at all.

Gradually, almost insensibly, I began to relax.

What, after all, did my worries matter in the eternal scheme of things? Was this place another Oxford, like Dorothy Sayers's in *Gaudy Night,* where learning was the only important thing? Where human passions were of far less concern than additions, however obscure, to the sum total of human knowledge?

Well, perhaps. In the eternal scheme of things. But that idea had not kept Harriet Vane from working very hard to solve the nasty problem besetting her Oxford college. And it wasn't going to keep me from doing my damnedest to solve Kevin Cassidy's murder.

I had wandered aimlessly. Now I looked up to get my bearings. I had gone right across the campus, my feet automatically following their old direction, and found myself in front of the Biological Sciences Building.

I allowed myself a tear or two. Dear old Kevin. And

dear, dear Frank. What impression had they left on that building? Did the classrooms and laboratories, in some dim, inarticulate way, remember those two exemplary men? Did their friendly ghosts haunt the halls, inspiring those who came after them?

Those who came after them! Those who worked there now, doing their research, adding to the sum total of human knowledge. Something stirred in my mind. Was I about to get an idea?

I was. Eureka! Those current seekers after wisdom included, I remembered with excitement, an entomologist I knew very well, whose odd specialty was the study of maggots. An unattractive subject, one would think, but he—Stan Harrington—had contributed greatly to forensic science. He knew exactly how the life cycles of the nasty little creatures could help determine when someone died.

When, for example, Jerry died.

I couldn't get that information from the police, but I was willing to bet I could get it from Stan. If he wasn't the "bug man" Darryl had called in, he'd know who was, and he'd get me the information.

Relieved, and suddenly exhausted, I took the shortest route back to the hotel, curled up gratefully against Alan's back, and went instantly to sleep.

I DIDN'T WAKE UNTIL midmorning, and then I talked Alan into going to lunch with me and Sharon. "Sharon's dying to meet you. And we need something to talk about, now that the Boland lead doesn't look at all promising."

Neither of us, truth to tell, went into the Administration Building with much enthusiasm. Square one is not a pleasant place to remain, nor a place to which one enjoys returning. I had told Alan about my ploy to gain information about Boland, though it now seemed likely to be pointless. My eagerness to talk to Stan Harrington had also ebbed. I'd also told Alan all about that, of course. But now, on a muggy, unseasonable morning with a thunderstorm threatening at any moment, my spirits had sagged again, and it didn't seem like such a hot idea.

"He probably won't know anything, either. Or he'll refuse to help. Or he'll have retired."

"You're cross because you didn't get enough sleep," Alan observed. "A walk will do you good."

"We have to take the car; we're taking Sharon to a place across town. And I am not cross!"

He was wise enough not to smile.

Sharon was waiting for us when we got to her office. She shook hands with Alan. "I can't wait to get to know you better, and I'll be right with you. If you'll just have a seat for a minute, I have to take these reports across the hall," she said. She gave me a broad wink and sailed briskly out the door with a pile of computer printouts.

"I suppose I might as well," I said in answer to Alan's raised eyebrow. "I'm here."

Sharon had considerately left Boland's file on top of the small stack on her desk. I opened it and flipped through quickly.

His transcript from undergraduate school. An excellent record, almost straight A's. His transcript from Johns Hopkins. Also excellent. I frowned. "There's nothing here to lead to anything at all. He was an almost perfect student."

Alan made a noncommittal noise.

"Wait, how did this get in here? It's a vitae. He must have applied for a job with the university—the health center, I suppose—and somehow this got in his student file, instead. The great bureaucracy at work.''

''May I see?''

''Sure. This stuff isn't even confidential, though the student records are supposed to be.''

Alan skimmed the document and then looked more closely at the second page. ''Hmmm.'' He ran a hand down the back of his head.

''What? Something interesting?''

''I think so.'' He pointed.

It took me a moment to see it, and when I did, I looked up, puzzled. ''There's a gap, isn't there? You don't notice it at first, but he left the hospital in Virginia in '94 and didn't start at the Ohio one until '95. That could be a matter of a month or two, or—''

''Or almost two whole years, depending on which month in each year. All the other dates are contiguous.''

''That might be worth checking, then. Let me just copy down the names of those hospitals, and maybe I can find out—''

''Hurry!''

I made a very quick note and was just slipping the vitae back into the folder when Sharon returned to the office. She carefully kept her back to us, fussing over a file cabinet, until I'd had time to align the folder neatly on her desk and stand up.

''Good. Ready to go? I ought to warn you I'm starving. I hope you brought lots of money.''

We enjoyed our lunch, but the tiny hint of mystery had revived my interest, and I was glad when we dropped Sharon back at her office, or as close as we could come in the car. ''This was fun; thank you. You must keep in touch, Dorothy, especially if anything exciting turns up in your life.'' She grinned conspiratorially and walked away, brisk as ever.

"Nice woman,'' Alan commented.

"The registrar's office—or whatever they're calling it now—would fall down without her. I always thought so, and one of her underlings said just that yesterday.''

"I trust she won't get into trouble for helping us.''

"She was very careful not to help us. It's not her fault if a couple of visitors who might be expected to behave just happen to snoop in a file when she's out of the office. But she'll want to know all about it if it turns out the information was a help. Myself, I can't figure out if it means anything or not.''

"It depends on specific dates. It may mean nothing at all except that he decided to give himself a brief vacation between jobs. However, he didn't stay very long in Ohio, either, did he?''

"Hmm. That's a point. You know, I wonder just how much Doc Foley knows about him? Do doctors check on each other at all, I wonder? Or does the AMA, or somebody? Or do they just take each other at face value?''

Alan shrugged. "Your health care system here works on such different principles from ours, I can't even guess.''

"Well, I suppose I should know, but in fact I don't. I can ask Doc. Meanwhile, would you like to learn a little about maggots, or is it too close to lunchtime?''

"My dear, I already know more about them than I wish I did. However, learning a bit more will not ruin my digestive processes.''

"It may well ruin mine, but anything for the cause. Let's go see the bug man.''

We drove to the nearest visitor parking lot. It was not

a good day for walking. The air had grown even closer and more humid; heavy clouds began to tower in the west. Dull thunder rumbled, distant but nearing. I wished the storm would hurry up and get it over with.

The university had not, as yet, found it necessary to alter the Biological Sciences Building. It was one of the older buildings on campus, but a new laboratory wing had been added in the 1970s. It might have been better, but it served. I hoped that when they did decide more modern facilities were required, they'd simply build a whole new lab and leave the old building alone.

Foolish romanticism, I told myself. But this place held memories for me.

The memories were a little too insistent when I approached the building. I detoured and entered by a side door. "Closer to Stan's lab," I explained to Alan.

And farther away from Frank's old office.

We found Stan happily engaged with a tray of what looked, at first sight, like swollen grains of rice.

"Hi!" he greeted us, as if I'd last seen him five minutes ago, instead of several years. "Want to watch the maggot races?"

"Stan, it's good to see you again. This is my husband, Alan Nesbitt." I didn't offer to shake hands, just in case…well, just in case. Neither, I noticed, did Alan. "Still absorbed in your work, I see."

"Well, sure." He sounded surprised. What else, after all, would a person do with his time? "I heard you were in town. Tough about Kevin, huh?"

"Very. Listen, Stan, I'm sure the maggot races are fascinating, but I need some information, if you have it. You know about Jerry—" I stopped. I still didn't know Jerry's last name. I looked at Alan, who shrugged and shook his head. "Well, Jerry. The rather odd man who lived in the woods close to Kevin?"

"And got himself bumped off. Sure. What do you want to know?"

"Have the police called you in to determine the time of death?"

"Sure. Who else?"

"Who else, indeed. So when did he die? Could you tell?"

The wonderful thing about Stan is that his curiosity is confined entirely to the behavior of insects. It would never occur to him to wonder why I wanted to know.

"Child's play. Anybody could have told them. They had some crazy idea he died Saturday night. No way. Monday morning. Ten or so. I couldn't pin it down to the minute, but before noon, absolutely. I'd say ten, myself."

The mobile grains of rice did something of apparent interest. "Hey, you sure you don't want to see this? It's terrific!"

I'd had rice with my lunch. I now regretted it. "Thank you, Stan, but another time. I have just one more question. What did Jerry die *of?*"

"Not my department," said Stan, "but it was obvious enough. Cherry red blood, you know."

"Cyanide, or carbon monoxide?" asked Alan.

"Cyanide, for sure. Killed some of the bugs. Hey, look at those little guys!"

I tried hard not to. "Great, Stan. And thanks for your help. We'll be on our way."

"Sure." He'd forgotten us by the time we reached the door.

TWENTY

FAT DROPS OF RAIN were beginning to fall when we left the lab. We made it to the car before the deluge, but only just. I hadn't fastened my seat belt before the storm arrived in full fury, the rain pelting the car like stones, the thunder and lightning almost continuous.

We waited it out. There was nothing else to do. I couldn't drive when I couldn't see. The wind howled and shook the car as it stood helpless against the elements.

"It was," Alan observed when the atmospherics abated a little, "a dark and stormy night."

"Afternoon. It only looks like night." A flash of lightning and a crack of thunder arrived simultaneously. I yelped and grabbed Alan's hand. "Did you see that? It struck the ground right there in front of us!"

"A car is quite a safe place during a storm, you know."

"I know that. You know that. But does the *lightning* know that?"

It didn't last long, of course. Storms like that wear themselves out quickly. The fireworks moved off, the rain slowed, the wind quieted. I didn't move. Alan looked at me with a question on his face.

"We might just as well stay here until it's really over. There'll be branches down after a storm like that, some streets will be flooded, some traffic lights will be out. It might be just as easy to leave the car here and walk, actually. But I'm not moving until the rain stops."

"Ah."

We sat listening to the rain.

"Cyanide," I said after a few minutes.

"Yes. Interesting, isn't it?"

"I don't think I expected that."

"Nor did I. I expected something a trifle more amateurish."

"A doctor would find it easy to get hold of cyanide."

"Still harping on Boland, are you? Dorothy, anyone would find it easy to get cyanide, if he put his mind to it. It's one of the most readily available poisons. Used in photography, industrial plating—oh, all sorts of things. The odd thing, to me, is that someone thought of it. Amateurs usually think of arsenic, if they think of poison at all."

"Well, I still think Boland is in the running. Maybe Kevin's stolen tricycle wasn't part of the pattern at all."

"You could be right. What do you plan to do about it?"

"I'm going to follow up that odd little gap in his employment record. I'm sure the university library will have computers for student use. I intend to surf the Net."

Alan's eyes twinkled. It wasn't so long ago that I took the normal middle-aged attitude toward computers— mysterious machines, somewhat threatening, often nuisances. It took a boy in his twenties to show me the possibilities; since then I've embraced the technology. When I want to learn more about almost any subject, I turn automatically to the Sherebury library's computers.

"And the best of luck, my dear. I think I'll strike out on my own. This cyanide business has made me more eager than ever to make Darryl an ally rather than an antagonist.''

"Why's that?''

"For one thing, cyanide is not a means I would expect a policeman to use to dispatch anyone. Especially an American policeman.''

My brows furrowed over that one for a moment, but then I got it. "Oh. Because American policemen have nice big fat guns on their hips. You think they would shoot, if they found murder necessary.''

"Well—let's say I think those big fat guns predispose one to violence. One's thoughts would turn to violent means. Not shooting, actually. It would be wildly stupid for a policeman to murder someone with his own gun, and Darryl is not stupid. Simply some violent method. And the second reason I'd like to clear Darryl, as soon as possible, is that the police have resources to trace the purchase of cyanide. They are in fact already doing so, almost certainly. It would be nice not to have to duplicate those efforts. It's stopped raining, by the way.''

"So it has. All right, we have a plan of action, at least for the time being. Look, the library's not far from here. Why don't I walk over there, and you take the car wherever you're going. Can you drive on the right, do you think?''

He grinned. "I think I might be able to manage for a street or two in a town this size.''

"Okay, I'll see you back at the hotel. I'll bet I find out more than you do!''

I splashed back across campus to the library in high spirits. The storm had left the air clean and fresh, and so brisk I was glad of the Burberry I'd been lugging around all day. The blue of the sky was beginning to win over the gray of the clouds by the time I dodged the largest of the puddles in front of the library door and went in.

The library seemed dark when I went in, nothing like as well lighted as I remembered. When I went to the information desk and asked about computer terminals, I realized why.

"All our computers are down, ma'am," said the young man at the desk, in the weary tone of one who has repeated the same statement too many times. He looked me over, gray hair, hat, and all, and explained further. "The storm took out our power and the modem lines. We're operating under emergency power. No, I don't know when they'll be back up. No, sir," to the man behind me, "they're all down. No, nobody's said when—"

I moved out of the way. Very well, the new technology was unavailable. I'd fall back on the old way: books.

I turned back to the harried young man at the desk. "Excuse me, but do you still have telephone books for other cities?"

"Over there." He pointed. "They're out of date, though. We use the computer now."

"No, you don't actually use the computer now, do you?" I retorted and turned away.

It took only a few minutes to look up a hospital in Richmond, Virginia, and one in Youngstown, Ohio. It took a little longer to find the American Medical Association publication that outlined certification procedures. Fortunately I knew the layout of the Randolph library far better than the student assistants, who were helpless when the computer catalogue wasn't operating. I'd never had occasion to use the medical reference section before, but I was able to find it.

Now for some phone calls. If the modem lines were

out at the library, the regular phone lines probably would be, too, and anyway pay phones are uncomfortable for anything more than the "I arrived safely; I'll see you in an hour" sort of thing. I started to walk back to the hotel, but on the way I changed my mind and detoured to Hillsburg Community Hospital. I might be able to find a shortcut.

The volunteers at the visitor desk were busy. Good. They wouldn't want to waste time with me.

"I don't want to keep you," I said guilelessly when a pleasant gray-haired man asked if he could help me. "Could I just see your staff directory for a minute? I used to know several people who worked here, and I'd like to say hello, but I've been out of town for a while, and I'm not sure which ones are still here."

I had the well-worn paperbound booklet in my hands before I'd even finished my explanation. Maybe they always let people look at it, but I hadn't wanted to take chances.

My excuse had been absolutely accurate, as far as it went. I was sure there were still a good many of my friends working here. I hadn't a clue, though, who they might be. I leafed through the booklet quickly.

Ahah! Not one but two former students of mine in the first two pages! One was working in human resources, what I always used to call personnel.

With access to computers.

"Thanks so much!" I handed the booklet back. "Where is the human resources department?"

"Second floor south," said one of the volunteers. "Take that elevator and turn left."

And there, at the end of the hall when I took the elevator and turned left, was a small office, one of several. In it sat Ray McKenzie, as red-headed and freckled as he had been in the fourth grade, and almost as round and rosy-cheeked.

The corridor was deserted. Nobody would notice if I paused a moment. I studied him, remembering him a little better now that he was in front of me. I would perhaps have done better to choose someone other than Ray. Ray had been a plump, serious little boy, not much given to mischief. Not exactly the star of his class. Somewhat slow over long division, as I recalled. And no good at all at any playground games. But he'd liked me. I'd worked with him until he actually enjoyed the intricacies of arithmetic. I'd also done my best to protect him from the small cruelties the others had imposed, almost unconsciously, on the child who was a little different, who didn't make friends easily.

He would remember me, I felt sure. It had only been a few years—well, ten—twelve? thirteen?—since he'd been in my class. Whether he, the serious, the hardworking, would help me with a somewhat unorthodox request was another matter.

I was here now. I couldn't lose anything by asking.

He was still as nearsighted as ever, his glasses still as thick. He looked up from his keyboard at my approach, but his eyes didn't focus on me.

"The employment office is by the elevators, back down the hall," he said, and turned back to his work.

"I've come to see you, Ray."

It took him a minute. Then he smiled and stood up to shake my hand. (He was always a polite child.)

"Mrs. Martin? I'm sorry I didn't recognize you at first, but—"

"But I'm the very last person you expected to see."

"Well, yeah. I mean—you're not applying for a job, are you?"

I laughed. "No, I've been retired for years, and I don't know what I could do in a hospital anyway."

Ray nodded, but he looked puzzled.

I had planned some small talk. Came by to see you, wondered how you were getting along, oh, by the way, there's something you could do for me.

It wasn't going to work with Ray. He didn't have the imagination to buy into an elaborate fiction.

"Actually, I do have a reason for being here. One of the doctors has disappeared."

"Oh, yeah, Dr. Boland. Everybody's talking about it. I even got to hear about it up here in my cubicle."

"Ray, I have some ideas about why he disappeared. I can't go into them now, but I'm one of those trying to find him."

"Why?"

"I can't tell you that, either. But you could be a big help to me, if you would."

His brow furrowed. "How?"

"It looks like your computer's working all right. The ones over at the university are all down. Is this one just internal, or will it access the Internet?"

"I only use it for staff records."

"I know that, but *could* you use it to get on the Net?"

"Well, sure. It's a terminal like all the rest."

"There's a national database for doctors' records. Their own records, I mean, not their patients'. Do you know how to get into that, or is it confidential?"

"No—no, I don't think so. I mean, yeah, I can get in it. I don't, much, but I can. And no, it isn't confidential. Anyhow, nobody ever told me it was."

"That was the impression I got, too. I have to tell you I just read up about this at the library, so I don't know much about it myself. Ray, you'd be doing me a real favor if you'd look up Dr. Boland for me."

Ray, would you like to clean the blackboard for me? Ray, could you take this message to the office? Oh, Ray, thank you! You did a beautiful job straightening that cupboard.

And Ray would tuck his chin into his collar and mumble something, and go back to his desk looking mildly pleased.

"We-ell..."

"I wouldn't ask if it weren't important. I don't know anybody else who could do this for me. I gather not just anyone has the access."

He sat up a little straighter. "Well, I guess it's okay. You wouldn't ask me to do something that wasn't. But I'm not sure how—I'll have to look it up." He opened a drawer and pushed the crowded contents around, finally coming up with a rather grubby pamphlet titled "A Guide to HCH Data Systems."

I longed to take it from him and find the instructions myself. He was still a slow reader. I managed to hide my impatience while he read a section aloud and put the information into action.

It was all worth it, though. When he finally negotiated the complexities of logging on to the database, and finally found Jim Boland's file, he let out a whistle.

"Gosh!"

"What? What did you find?"

"Gosh, he's been in a lot of trouble!"

He swiveled the monitor up and around so that I could see.

There it was. Dr. Boland's guilty past. The malpractice suits, the judgments against him, the out-of-court settlements. The information he was required to report when requesting residency in any hospital.

"Can you print it out for me?"

"Sure. Gosh, though! Whoever would've thought?" He handed me the printouts.

"Ray, this is just what I needed. You've been an enormous help!"

"Gee, I'm glad I could help. This is all kind of exciting, huh?"

"It is, indeed. But Ray—our secret for now, right?"

"Right!" He grinned shyly at me, tucked his chin into his collar, and went back to his work, looking mildly pleased.

TWENTY-ONE

I WALKED STRAIGHT TO Doc Foley's office.

"Do you have an appointment?"

"No, and it's not a medical emergency, but I need to see him, just for a few minutes. Tell him I'm here, will you? And tell him it's about Dr. Boland. I'll be glad to wait."

The office was full, as it almost always was. Doc was the sort of doctor who made you feel, when you got into his office, that he had nothing more important to do than listen to you tell him just what the trouble was. That, combined with the fact that he never refused a new patient who was really sick, and the only way his old patients ever left him was in a coffin (despite his best efforts), meant that you usually had to wait.

Thus I was not popular when, about five minutes later, the nurse called me in ahead of at least three people.

"I'm sorry," I said to all and sundry. "I really won't be a minute."

None of them looked any happier.

He was waiting for me at his desk. "This better be good, kid."

"I know. You have an office full of patients ready to lynch me. Doc, look at this."

I pulled the printouts out of my purse.

He read them, looked up at me, read them more carefully, and finally laid them on the desk. He pulled off his glasses, rubbed the corners of his eyes, and sighed.

"Well? How did a man like that ever get a practice in Hillsburg?"

"Appearances can be deceiving, you know. Some of these cases may not be anything like as serious as they look."

"He caused an aortal aneurysm, Doc! He made a hole—well, almost—in somebody's aorta, for Pete's sake! The poor woman's probably an invalid for life, and it was supposed to be just a routine angioplasty!"

"Aneurysms can almost always be repaired, Dorothy. And doctors are human. We make mistakes. Oh, we'd like to pretend it isn't so, but accidents happen. One accident doesn't mean somebody's a bad doctor, just that he was unlucky."

"Not as unlucky as the patient," I said tartly. "And there's sure more than one in this record."

He looked at it again. "Hmmm. The illegible prescriptions—common enough, but careless, certainly. The forgotten allergy—that's more serious. Dorothy, I'm not saying Boland is a man I would have chosen for Hillsburg, if I'd known about all this."

"But you didn't."

I must have sounded accusing, because I could hear the effort it took Doc not to lose his temper.

"Dorothy, I don't sit on the credentials board. I can't personally check up on every doctor who wants to practice in this town. There's a shortage of doctors willing to serve as family practitioners in a small town."

"Now, see, that's another thing I don't understand. Why Hillsburg? He's kept on going to smaller and smaller towns. And why did he change from his cardiac specialty to family practice?"

"Oh, that's easily explained. After the angioplasty that went wrong in Virginia, he probably wanted to get out of cardiology. So he took some courses, boned up on family practice, and went to a smaller town in Ohio. Apparently he had some problems there, too, so he came to us."

"And Kevin died."

"Now, look here, Dorothy! Once and for all, get it out of your head that Kevin died because of Boland's care! He did everything anyone could. How many more times—?"

"Then why did he leave town?"

Doc was silent.

"Doc, I know I'm being a pest, and your patients are going to lose their patience in about a minute. Just tell me one thing. Who could have known about his record?"

"Anyone with access to that database. It's fairly expensive to subscribe to, but every hospital has access, and most big clinics. We share information."

"But not to laymen."

"Well—laymen could get to it if they wanted to."

"They'd have to know about it."

"True."

After a moment I stood up and gave Doc my hand.

"Thanks. I haven't worked it all out yet, but this means something. And by the way, if you still want to, I think I know where to find Dr. Boland!"

I left him with that to think about.

I stretched out on the bed when I got back to the hotel, thinking to rest my back and knees and puzzle over my information. Alan woke me out of a sound sleep.

"Productive afternoon, love?"

I yawned and sat up, piling pillows behind my back.

"You can keep the sarcasm out of your voice, thank you. I had a very productive afternoon indeed, and I can't have been asleep more than half an hour. Anyway, I deserved a nap after last night's excursion. How about you? You look as though somebody's given you a present."

"I think you'll agree that somebody has. But I want to save it. Tell me what you've learned."

I told him, leaving out no detail.

"The guilty secret," he said when I had finished. "The only trouble being that it's not a secret at all."

"Well, that is a problem. But I'm not sure it's such a big one. Sure, the Hillsburg Hospital people certified him, or whatever the term is. They admitted him as a resident. Doc implied that they might have been pretty hard up for doctors and ready to take somebody whose record was more than a little doubtful. But what would have happened if there'd been a malpractice suit here, and the press had gotten hold of the thing? They could have. Newsmen know how to find out things; they probably know all about that database."

Alan shook his head slowly. After a moment I leaned back against the pillows and sighed. "It's not enough, is it?"

"It's not enough, I think, to make a motive for murder. Your idea, I take it, has been that Kevin found out and told Boland he would have to tell—tell whom?"

"I don't know. I suppose I had thought the hospital authorities. But of course they already knew. So..." I raised a hand and let it drop. "I guess I didn't accomplish anything this afternoon, after all."

"You settled the matter of Dr. James Boland for certain," Alan said calmly. "We now know why he left town."

"We do?"

"He left for the same reason he left Richmond and Youngstown, or almost the same. There hadn't been a malpractice suit yet, but he felt one was in the offing. He might have thought you planned to file one on Kevin's behalf. Whatever his reasoning was, he was certain that Hillsburg had become one more place where he could no longer practice medicine. So he left."

"But he didn't kill Kevin or Jerry. And we're no nearer knowing who did."

"You've eliminated one suspect. And I, my dear, have eliminated another."

I forgot my disappointment and sat up again. "You have! Who?"

He sat down on the edge of the bed. "Let me tell it my way. You told me I looked as though I'd been given a present. I feel that way, I admit. I went to talk to Father Kennedy, to see if I couldn't pin him down to some dates."

"The dates when things happened to Kevin?"

"Yes. He wasn't a great deal of help, actually, though he tried hard. I wasn't surprised. One doesn't remember the exact date when things happen, especially at an age when one's memory begins to be unreliable about everything."

I made a small noise of rueful agreement. "But you said you were able to eliminate one suspect. How, if you couldn't establish any more dates?"

Alan smiled with satisfaction. "I couldn't establish dates, no. But I did establish a connection. We talked, Father Kennedy and I, about all the incidents. I thought something might trigger a memory. We talked about the telephone problems, and I propounded my theory of how they might have been caused and where someone might have gotten the idea. We went from that to the fire, since the telephone, as you may remember, was out of order then. Father Kennedy said again that Kevin had managed to put it out himself before much harm had been done.

"And did the police investigate the fire? I asked him. Somehow neither you nor I had thought to ask that before. And he said—wait for it—he said that the police had been notified, but that nothing much had been done, because the police were overworked just then. The chief was on holiday, and nothing seemed to be going well for them."

He paused to watch my reaction. "The chief was on holiday! Only I bet Father Kennedy called it vacation. Where, did he know?"

"No, I asked him. But it was easy enough to find out."

"How?"

"I went to the police station and asked."

"You asked Darryl where he went on vacation? Alan, you didn't!"

He laughed and patted my knee. "No, I didn't. I asked that nice young officer who took care of Kevin's cats. Of course I didn't ask him, baldly, where his chief went for his holidays. I told him I had dropped in to ask after the cats. They're fine, by the way. Three of them have already been adopted."

"The little gray one?" I asked anxiously. "I liked her the best."

"Yes, the little gray one. That led to a discussion of his own cats, and I talked about ours, and the difficulty of arranging for their care when we went away. Of course, that made it natural to speak of journeys and traveling, so I mentioned that I didn't know this part of the country at all, and asked where the popular holiday spots were.''

I was the one who laughed at that. "And he told you there weren't any.''

"He was quite polite about it, said that people usually went to Disney World or Las Vegas. Pressed a bit, he said that he and his wife didn't like that sort of thing, that they would camp up in Michigan or walk the Appalachian Trail. Do you, by the way, know about the Appalachian Trail?''

"Not from personal experience," I assured him.

"Well, it doesn't sound the sort of thing a policeman would do voluntarily, at least not one who had walked a beat in his early days as I did. I told the officer that, and he laughed and said that his chief was of the same opinion. That, of course, gave me the opening I needed.''

"So you asked.''

"So I asked. And he told me that the chief, for his last three holidays—sorry, vacations—had taken his family to one of the national parks. Yosemite, Yellowstone, and the Grand Canyon were mentioned.''

I fell back against the pillows in relief. "So Darryl's out of it for sure.''

"It would certainly seem so. Unless, of course, the origin of the fire turned out to be electrical or some other accidental cause—'' He dodged the pillow I threw at him. "All right, all right! I don't really believe that. I believe we've exonerated the police chief. And I would suggest that our first call tomorrow morning be at the police station.''

TWENTY-TWO

"HO-KAY."

The remark, which quite obviously did not imply agreement, was Darryl's sole reaction the next morning to our story. He sat behind his desk, studying first one and then the other of us, his lips pursing in and out, his right hand playing with his pencil. The point bounced on the blotter. The eraser. The point.

Finally he tossed the pencil aside and cleared his throat. "I'm not sure I know what to say to all that. It's a first, anyway. Nobody ever accused me of murder before."

I started to say something, but Alan gave me a sharp look, and I subsided.

"Now lemme see if I got this straight. You think Kevin Cassidy was murdered, because he said in that note that somebody was out to get him."

"Not just in the note. His priest—"

This time Alan's look was an outright glare.

"And you think Jerry Briggs was killed because he knew something about Kevin's murder."

"Briggs? Was that his name?"

Darryl ignored me and looked at Alan, who said quietly, "Something of an oversimplification, but yes, that essentially is what we believe."

"Ho-kay," he said again. "Well, I'm glad you finally

decided to tell me about it. No"—he raised a hand as I tried again to speak—"it's okay. I see why you thought you couldn't say anything before. The question is, now what do you expect me to do about it?"

"Well—investigate it, of course! Share information, let us help!"

Darryl ignored me again and looked steadily at Alan.

"I've been very uncomfortable, sir, with the idea of withholding information from you. I hope you truly do understand our motives. Now that we are satisfied that we can speak freely, it seemed wise to let you know what we're doing. You are at perfect liberty to accept our story or not, and you are under no obligation to do anything about it whatever." He met Darryl's eyes levelly.

They reminded me of two strange cats. Any moment now one of them would hiss and raise a fully armed paw. I caught myself holding my breath.

It was Darryl who backed off. Sighing deeply, he picked up the pencil and began fiddling with it again. "Sorry. I guess you couldn't play it any other way. That is, if I believed a word of it, which I can't say I do. I mean, I believe that you believe it. I just can't buy it myself. Kevin Cassidy died of pneumonia, and that's it. As for Jerry—well, I admit I don't know why anybody would want to give him cyanide. What I figure is, nobody did—I mean not on purpose."

"You think it was an accident?" asked Alan in friendly fashion, one policeman to another.

"Not that way. I mean, I don't think he put cyanide in his coffee by mistake for sugar. No, I think we've got one of those maniacs on our hands. You know the capsule murders a few years ago, when somebody went around putting cyanide into medicine bottles in drugstores? He didn't care who he killed; he was a nut. And then somebody else did it to cover up the real murder he really wanted to commit?''

"His wife, as I recall."

"Right. Well, I'm scared stiff we've got another one of those loose around here."

"Hmm." Alan considered the possibility and raised an objection. "What about tamperproof packaging?"

"That only protects the people who are smart enough to take a bottle of pills back to the drugstore if the seal's broken. You think Jerry was that smart?"

"You have a point, at that. Do you mind telling me what steps you are taking?"

"We're going through Jerry's trailer with a fine-tooth comb, to start with. Trying to figure out what he might have taken, while the medical examiner's testing Jerry's stomach contents for everything he can think of. Sending everything we find in the trailer to the lab to be tested for traces of cyanide. And we've alerted the drugstores and grocery stores and every place else where people buy over-the-counter medicine. We can't go for a recall until we know what the stuff was in, so we just have to tell the stores to be on the lookout for anybody acting funny. And we're praying we can get it worked out before somebody else dies."

Alan nodded approvingly. "Very thorough. If you are dealing with a maniac, though, you'll need those prayers. The tests and so on take time."

"You're telling me. So you can see I don't have any time for any wild-goose chases."

Wild-goose chase. That was the metaphor Alan had used before we found out so much. Surely now, Darryl...

Alan smiled at me and pressed my hand. "No, I do

quite see that," he said, looking back at Darryl. "We won't take any more of that time. I take it you have no objection to our continuing our pursuits? Good. If we do learn anything of interest, about maniacs or anyone else, would you like to hear of it?"

"Sure, why not?" At the thought of getting us out of his hair, Darryl turned almost genial. "I guess you never know."

I turned to Alan when we were safely out on the sidewalk. He shrugged. "What did you expect? At least he offered no active hindrance."

"And that in itself is a help, I suppose."

"Well, yes, it is, but I rather expected you to be discouraged by his attitude."

"You don't agree with him, do you? About a maniac on the loose?"

"It's a possibility, certainly. A good policeman never ignores—"

"Oh, *don't* go all calm and reasonable and logical on me! Never mind what a good policeman should do. Whose side are you on, anyway?"

"Yours, my love, always yours."

"Well, then, I flatly refuse to be discouraged. I've spent too much time down in the dumps lately." I raised my head and took a deep breath. The air was like—no, not just wine, but champagne, clear and crisp and fragrant with the invigorating smell of dried leaves. The sky was that perfect deep October blue, with puffy little clouds painted in at exactly the most decorative spots. "It is a perfectly gorgeous, heaven-sent morning, and it's a sin for anybody to be discouraged on such a day. And I don't want to waste any more time. Come on!"

"Where are we going?"

"Where we should have gone ages ago. Where we

started to go before Jerry fended us off and we got distracted by all sorts of side issues. We're going to Kevin's house.''

Alan grinned, tucked my arm in his, and set a brisk pace back to our car.

When we got to Kevin's and I started to get out of the car, he cleared his throat. ''Umm—far be it from me to raise difficulties, but how are we to get in?''

''I told you he almost never locked his door. He must have been one of the last people on earth who trusted everybody.''

''Unwise.''

''Yes, as it turned out, but honestly, Alan, it must be a nice way to go through life.''

The door, however, was locked. Alan didn't seem surprised. ''His executor would have done that. Ms. Carmichael, presumably.''

''Darn! And we don't want to ask her for the key, do we? But wait a minute—I think I remember—'' I pulled up the cushion on one of the rocking chairs, and sure enough, there was a key.

Alan shook his head. ''The first place a burglar would look.''

''But Kevin didn't expect burglars. He only ever locked the doors when he was going to be away for a while and somebody else was taking care of the cats. He said they'd get upset about him leaving it open, so he locked it to please them, and then told them where to leave the key. Eccentric—but then, he was. Come on in.''

It seemed strange to walk into Kevin's house without him there to welcome me. The room was filled with sunshine and with Kevin. His presence was everywhere. His books filled and overflowed the bookshelves. His favorite leather chair, well worn, showed the impress of his body. His pipe, in a big ashtray, sat handy there on the arm of the chair.

"He never would give up his pipe," I said irrelevantly. "By the time everybody figured out how dangerous smoking was, he said he'd already outlived all his contemporaries, so he might as well enjoy his one vice."

"And he died of a lung problem."

It was a comment on the irony of life, no more; I dismissed it.

If I let myself, I could easily get sentimental and weepy, I thought, looking around the room. But I'd promised myself that my doldrums were past, and weeping wasn't going to fulfill my responsibility to Kevin. We'll figure it out, I promised him silently. We won't let them get by with it.

Alan had wandered out to the kitchen; now he rejoined me. "He was a good housekeeper, I see. Or did he have someone come in?"

There was in his voice that same note of surprise as when he had first seen the outside of the house.

"No, he did it all himself, and yes, he was comfortably untidy, but he was clean. Of course, the place hasn't been dusted for some time, but it was always nicely kept when he was—when he could look after it. I'm willing to bet he even made his bed after he got out of it"—I swallowed hard and continued—"to go to the hospital."

Alan checked and came back. "Right you are. He, or someone, made the bed. There's a bit of disorder in the room—medicines on the bedside table, that sort of thing—but then he expected to come home and tidy that away."

I blinked and dug my fingernails into the palms of my

hands. Physical pain, I've found, can often take one's mind off emotional pain.

I cleared my throat. "Alan, this is the place where your training is going to help a lot more than anything I can contribute. What are we looking for?"

"Anything at all unusual," he said promptly. "Any signs of an intruder. That's the sort of thing I might see more easily than you would. Anything that doesn't belong here, or anything missing that should be here. Anything out of character. Anything, no matter how insignificant, that seems in any way wrong. And that's where you'll be more useful than I."

"Are you sure? I haven't been in this house for years, Alan. I didn't have his belongings memorized."

"No, but you knew his character, his personality, some of his likes and dislikes. You knew about his pipe, for example. If there had been a pack of cigarettes in that ashtray, it wouldn't have surprised me, but it would have struck you as odd."

"Okay, I see what you mean. You'll look for the criminal stuff, and I'll look for the everyday stuff."

He grinned. "More or less. Shall we work together or separately?"

"Separately. Then we can compare notes."

So Alan began a minute examination of the doors and windows while I stood in the middle of the living room and just looked around me.

The books. Was anything missing?

Heavens, I didn't know what the man read. Technical books, of course. I knew enough, from Frank, about the basic biology texts that I could tell they were all there. There were also a lot of far more esoteric ones on the shelves. I knew nothing about them and couldn't even guess whether the collection was complete.

I moved to the shelves of lighter books. Nothing struck me as out of character. He didn't read best-sellers, as a rule, so *Snow Falling on Cedars* was perhaps a little unexpected, but that was such a marvelous book, anybody would have enjoyed it. There wasn't much recent fiction, but a number of classics: Dickens, Conrad, Jane Austen, Mark Twain. A selection of history, biography, philosophy, some of the better-known works of lay theology. A few general reference works: an atlas, an unabridged dictionary, an encyclopedia. For specific reference, he would have relied on the university library.

That reminded me. I searched the shelves a little more closely and found, sure enough, a bottom shelf stacked with library books to be returned. Some from the public library, some from the university. Overdue now, of course. I supposed the post office had sent the overdue notices back to the libraries. Was there a rubber stamp for "deceased"? I shuddered and made a mental note to take the books with us when Alan and I left. We could at least do that tiny thing for Kevin, if nothing else.

The bookshelves didn't seem helpful. I wandered over to Kevin's pride and joy, the woodstove, and peered behind it. It was set away from the fieldstone chimney wall by a careful eighteen inches, and I had some vague idea something might be hidden back there. There was nothing, of course, except evidence that here his standard of housekeeping had fallen somewhat short. The back of the stove was blistered where the black finish had apparently burned off, and the hardwood floor beyond the back edge of the tiled hearth was also scarred and blistered. The heat had been too intense, perhaps? And Kevin had never noticed, and now he could never repair the damage.

I worked my way around the room. The furniture

wasn't in pristine condition. Kevin had loved it and lived
with it for decades. It looked much as usual, however.
Lamps, curtains, old radio, record player. Kevin had no
television and had never bothered with advancements in
music reproduction; the LP was good enough for him.
He liked jazz, I seemed to remember—yes, there were
the jazz records, a few big band recordings, remastered
from the originals of the 1930s and '40s, a sprinkling of
light classics. I turned on the radio just to check the
station; nothing happened. Oh, of course, the electricity
would have been shut off. Who had seen to that? I wondered. Ms. Carmichael, probably.

A magazine rack held professional journals, a sprinkling of catalogues, several issues of *Smithsonian,* a
Time from mid-August.

A sturdy rolltop desk held paid bills. The unpaid ones
had presumably been taken away by the lawyer. There
were letters marked "answered" and two or three that
would remain forever unanswered. I glanced through
them, feeling distinctly uneasy. A lady does not read
someone else's mail. But they were routine, all of them,
chatty letters from friends still too old-fashioned to prefer the telephone. There was no question of e-mail.
Kevin didn't own a computer.

It saddened me that there was no work in progress. I
had never known Kevin when he wasn't working on
some learned paper or other. But he'd given up his work
in the lab. He'd had nothing to write about.

There was only one painting on the wall, a big oil of
some zinnias in a blue glass bowl, done years ago by a
local artist, Kevin had told Frank and me. It was a lovely
thing. I wondered if it would look nice in Mary Alice's
house and if she would like to have it. I wouldn't ask

her; she resented me. But I'd try to remember to mention it to the lawyer.

That seemed to be it for the living room. I made a methodical search of the kitchen—no food, but otherwise as usual, I'd guess. And the food would have been removed by whoever had taken such thoughtful care of other details. Whoever they were, they'd missed only the library books.

I had to steel myself to enter the bedroom, but it, too, was in apparently normal condition. I'd been in it once or twice, probably—guests used to put their coats on the bed—but I remembered almost nothing about it. It all looked normal to me, as did the bathroom. The bathroom cabinet, with its lethal potential, I left to Alan. Criminal matters were his department. I went on looking for something out of the ordinary.

And I didn't find it. I exhausted the possibilities in the main house at about the same time that Alan pronounced himself finished, so we went out together to the shed that had served as Kevin's workshop.

"I've never seen any of this before," I reminded Alan. "He built this after I left town. So I can't be any help at all."

"Do you know anything about stained glass?"

"Nothing whatever, except that I like it, at least when it's as well done as Kevin's."

"You know," said Alan, running a hand down the back of his neck, "I have a nagging feeling there's something odd about this stained-glass business."

"Odd how? You can't mean Kevin was up to something shady?"

"No, no. It simply seems to—crop up. So many people had some of Kevin's projects. So many people visited him with commissions shortly before his death. And

there's something else—something—'' He took off his
glasses and massaged the bridge of his nose, as if he
could rub it, like a lamp, and the genie of his missing
idea would appear. "No," he said at last. "It's gone.
I'd best leave it alone; it'll surface if I don't try to think
of it. Let's see what we can find."

We looked around. The workshop, small but adequate,
looked like the rest of Kevin's domain, slightly untidy
but essentially clean. Small sheets of glass in jewel colors lay on their sides in padded racks against one wall.
Rolls of copper foil tape and solder were stacked on the
workbench. Glass cutters, pencils, and colored marking
pens stood upright in an old, dimpled English beer mug.
A small stack of face masks, the kind dentists and nurses
use, lay next to it. Two stacks of graph paper, one un-
used, one with designs drawn on the sheets, were neatly
lined up on one corner of the bench. In the center lay
an unfinished project, a simple sun-catcher in a wavy
pattern and the colors of the sea, cerulean blue, tur-
quoise, aquamarine. A few pieces were lined up on top
of the corresponding parts of the pattern; the rest were
yet to be cut. I couldn't bear to look at it.

There was nothing unusual at all. Alan examined everything twice and then shook his head.

"Whatever it was I expected to find, it isn't here."
He looked at me carefully and put his arm around my
shoulders. "And you've had as much as you can take,
love. Let's go back to the hotel, and you can cry all you
want."

TWENTY-THREE

I DID CRY. I lay on the bed and bawled, but this time it wasn't out of depression or frustration. It was for Kevin and the waste of the good years he'd still had left, for the poignancy of the unanswered letters, the unread books, the unfinished beauty he'd left behind. When I'd gotten it out of my system, I sat up, blew my nose, and straightened my hair.

"There. That's that. I couldn't help it, but I'm over it now, and I'll shed no more tears for dear Kevin. He wouldn't like it; he hated to see women cry. What I need to do now—what we need to do—is go back to the notebooks and see what we've got."

"No, what we need to do is find some lunch. Do you realize it's long past noon?"

"Oh. That would account for the hollow feeling. I thought it was just grief."

We split a stromboli sandwich—Alan had become addicted to them—and then got right back to the hotel and to work.

"Did you find anything unusual at Kevin's house?" I sat down at the table and opened the notebook to a fresh page.

"All my evidence is negative. There were no signs of forced entry. I'd have been surprised to find any, of course, since he didn't lock his doors. I could see no signs of a search, either. No one came in to find the hidden jewels, or the treasure map, or even the stash of cocaine.''

I looked up from the notebook, startled. ''Alan! What stash of cocaine?''

''The one that no one came looking for, because it didn't exist. Nothing was hidden anywhere, so far as I could tell without taking the place apart. There wasn't even a gun or any ammunition, which is perhaps a little unusual for an American living alone, out in the country.''

''My dear prejudiced Englishman! We're not all armed to the teeth. I told you Kevin tried to live in harmony with nature. He didn't like guns.''

''Ah, yes, you did say that. Full marks to Kevin. I also studied the telephone wires rather carefully, but could find no sign, inside the house or out, of tampering.''

''Oh. Does that mean the phone problems were accidental? Nothing to do with our villain?''

''Possibly. Or, more probably, he or she found some more subtle way to disrupt Kevin's service.''

''Like what?''

''My dear, I am not an expert on the subject. It did look as though the wires had been in place for quite some time, so they are presumably old-fashioned coaxial cable rather than modern fiber optics. In that case I would guess that something as simple as a sturdy pin, inserted into the cable in exactly the right spot so as to touch both wires, would short out the system.''

''And then the pin could be taken out again and everything would go back to normal?''

''I don't know. That would depend on the nature of the system and, as I have said, I'm no expert. Certainly a pin, or even a narrow brad, would leave little trace of its having been there, only a very tiny hole in the insulation. Unless one were looking for such a thing, it would pass unnoticed.''

"And were you looking for a hole?''

"I was not." Alan grinned. "I only just thought of it, if you want the truth. I was looking for evidence of criminal activity, and I found nothing significant, save to eliminate the obvious. And you, my dear Miss Pinkerton?''

I smiled to myself. So he read Mary Roberts Rinehart. I was learning things about my husband on this trip. "Nothing much. He hadn't blacked his stove lately. Some of the finish was gone, on the back, and there were some funny stains on the floor there, too. I suppose they were burn marks, although Kevin was always very careful about making sure the stove was safe. He was a real expert on Franklin stoves. Maybe he spilled something and never got a chance to clean it up. Oh, and the library books. Darn, I forgot to bring the library books back with us." I explained about the books.

"Well, we can always go back. I ought to take a look at those stains, just so we can cross them off our list.''

I made a couple of brief entries and then turned back to the beginning of the notebook.

"We can fill in a lot of this, now. Let's go to work.''

We worked solidly for an hour, condensing, summarizing, now and then adding a note. When we had finished, I looked at the results, yawned, and flexed my shoulders.

"All right. We progress. Jerry is eliminated, poor dear—in every sense. Darryl and Dr. Boland are eliminated because they were out of town at material times. Darn it, I regretted drawing that line through Boland's name! If ever a man deserved to be convicted of *something,* he does.''

"At least it means we needn't take in the opera tomorrow night."

"Oh, yes, we do! I want to give the man a piece of my mind. He may not be guilty of Kevin's death, or Jerry's, but he's guilty of a lot of other unpunishable crimes.''

Alan rolled his eyes to the ceiling and sighed.

"So that leaves Michelle Carmichael, Hannah Schneider, Mary Alice Harrison, and that miserable excuse for a preacher, Bob Bussey."

We studied their entries carefully.

"Michelle Carmichael. Briskly efficient, discreet, probably borrowed money from Kevin.''

"We don't know that, Dorothy."

"That's why I said 'probably.' I still think she did, though. There was something about the way she carefully didn't say anything. Okay, moving on. Hannah Schneider. Fanatic, extremely busy. Ordered stained glass from Kevin. He donated to her cause.''

"And she didn't want to talk about the stained glass!'' said Alan triumphantly. "I knew there was something about the glass. That's it. Hannah didn't mention she'd been there recently, remember?''

"Vaguely. But I honestly think she just forgot. Goodness knows she has enough irons in the fire to make anybody forget something minor like that.''

I waited, but Alan made no reply, so I went ahead.

"Mary Alice Harrison. A bitter woman, but no motive to kill Kevin. She doesn't inherit.''

"Ah, but wait a minute. When did she know she didn't inherit? Did she go to the solicitor before or after Kevin died?''

I thought about that. "After," I said slowly. "Because she said something about not wanting to bother him for money, but once he had no further use for it...something like that."

"So she didn't know that there was no money for her until after he was dead."

We considered that for a moment. I made a note. "But, Alan, that poor woman—two small children and another on the way..."

"Mothers will do what is necessary to protect their young," he said gently.

I sighed. "All right, you've made your point, but my money is still right here." I pointed to the chart, now a spidery mess of arrows and interlinings and obliterations.

"Dear old Parson Bob? On what grounds?"

"On the grounds, first, that I can't stand him, and second, he's the type who would kill his grandmother and make it sound like he ought to get a medal for it, and third, he didn't like Kevin. He's the only one we've talked to who didn't, you realize. Besides, he looks like every movie villain you've ever seen on the late show, and I don't care if my reasoning is way off in left field, I think we ought to go over there and ask him some very pointed questions. It's probably too late today, but first thing tomorrow. A little harassment of a sanctimonious phony sounds like a lovely way to spend a morning, don't you think?"

"It has its attractions, I admit. Very well. First agenda item for tomorrow: the questionable cleric."

PARSON BOB, it turned out, didn't live next door to the church as one might expect. We drove out there on Thursday morning and found no one home at the tiny house next to the cemetery; the name on the mailbox

was "Stoner." The church itself was locked up tight
with no one around. A phone booth at a nearby gas
station actually had a phone book in it, by some miracle,
but Bob Bussey wasn't listed. "Hmph!" I snorted. "Un-
listed number for a pastor. Fine minister to his flock he
must be!"

"Yes, well, we had already deduced that. Dare we ask
our good friend the police chief?"

"Let's try the library first. They'll have a city directory."

We found him there, with a five-digit address on a
street called Hummingbird Way. "Never heard of it. It'll
be in one of those new subdivisions; I'll need a map."

The house turned out to be a painfully new one, raw
red brick with a broad, gleaming concrete driveway. It
was ostentatious without being in any way beautiful, its
impact being one of sheer size. Three-car garage, double
front doors, huge bay window, wings and ells and
porches and extensions. Its harsh newness was softened
by no plantings; even the grass was not yet well established. As we approached, the larger of the two garage
doors started to slide up, and we heard a car engine start.

"Quick, Dorothy! Pull into the drive."

I obeyed, situating our car carefully so that whichever
car was about to go out, the way would be blocked. And
then I saw the big Lincoln start to move.

I thought for one awful moment that the preacher
wasn't even going to look, and I had visions of extensive
repairs to our uninsured rental car. However, the big
black car traveled only a few inches before it stopped.
The car door slammed, and a furious parson charged out
of the garage.

"You'll have to move your car, whoever—oh. It's
you. Well, I'm just leaving, as you might have noticed

if you'd been paying attention. I have an important call to make, so you'll have to come back later if you want to talk to me."

"We do want to talk to you," said Alan, getting out of the car with surprising speed. There was no trace of his usual amiability on his face or in his voice. "And I'm afraid it will have to be now."

"What do you mean? Who do you think you are, bossing me around? You're trespassing, I'll have you know!"

His private manner was certainly different from the one he employed in front of his congregation.

"You know that my name is Alan Nesbitt," said my husband, still in that hard voice. "I don't believe I told you that I was the principal law enforcement officer for the county of Belleshire."

Oh, bravo Alan! I didn't think Parson Bob, whose pale complexion was now a nasty shade of green, would notice Alan's careful use of the past tense. Nor was he apt to question where in the world Belleshire was.

I sat back to enjoy the show.

"And what does that have to do with me?" The bluster had diminished considerably.

Alan ignored the question. "I'm very interested in the money that you say Kevin Cassidy gave you shortly before his death. I believe it amounted to several thousand dollars?"

"I—no! I didn't say that! And it was a loan, not a gift."

"I see. You paid it back."

"No, of course not. He died before my congregation—"

"Ah, it would have been your *congregation* who took the responsibility for repaying the loan."

"Well, of course! The money was to be used for the benefit of the church."

"'Was to be'? How has it in fact been used?" Alan allowed his eyes to linger on the huge, expensive car, the huge, expensive house.

"I don't know who you think you are, but if you're accusing me—"

"I have accused you of nothing. I am simply asking questions. I presume that the account books of the church are available for inspection?"

"Oh, of course they are, Alan," I put in sweetly. "They have to be, after all. The church must be able to show its nonprofit status in order to keep its tax exemption."

"I have nothing to hide! From the proper authorities, that is. I'm doing God's work. If he has chosen to reward me according to my efforts on his behalf, I don't see how that's any business of yours. And where'd you say you're from, anyway?"

Alan chose to answer that obliquely. "I come, sir, from a place where we take seriously the matter of defrauding the elderly. Were you aware that Dr. Cassidy had nearly exhausted his resources? How do you suppose he would have lived once you had bilked him of his life savings?"

"That's an insult, and what's more, I don't believe a word of it! He was rolling in money. He gave me that five thou—that donation of his own free will. It's not my problem if he didn't have it to give. He never told me that! And there's always Medicaid. What do we pay taxes for, anyhow?" His voice had risen to a scream. Little drops of spittle appeared at the corners of his mouth.

Alan looked at him with disgust written all over his

face. The preacher clutched at the rags of his dignity and tried to take a higher tone. "God will always provide for his children, even those who have turned away from him, if they repent and mend their evil ways. I had every reason to believe that Mr. Cassidy's loan was intended to get him right with God." His control broke. "Now, get out of my driveway before I call the cops!"

"I think you will find that my wife and I are on very good terms with your police chief," said Alan, ice in his voice. "However, it seems almost a blasphemy to waste this lovely morning talking to you. Good day, sir."

He stepped back into the car and we drove off, leaving an angry and shaken parson standing in his gleaming new driveway, staring after us.

TWENTY-FOUR

"THAT IS," I SAID with precision, when we were well away, "the sorriest excuse for a human being it has ever been my misfortune to encounter."

"Quite," said Alan. Then he broke into a broad smile. "I've not enjoyed anything so much in years!"

"You were magnificent! You had him shaking in his boots. I wonder how much of his congregation's funds he has misappropriated over the years?"

"One also wonders whether he will continue his peculations, or whether I have, as it were, put the fear of God into him."

"I'm willing to bet he'll keep right on doing it until he gets caught. I think I may put in a call to the IRS when we get back to town."

"Now that," said Alan, patting my knee, "is retribution with a vengeance. What an excellent idea."

"Actually, though," I said after thinking about it for another mile or two, "I ought to give him a vote of thanks."

"Whatever for?"

"Because he did say something back there that I'm beginning to think might be important."

"I heard nothing but bluster and excuses."

"That's because you're not American. I may have had some difficulties pursuing an investigation on this side of the Atlantic, but I also have a few advantages. One is that I know about Medicaid.''

"Ah, yes, I recall the word. What, precisely, is Medicaid?''

I thought for a minute. "It's hard to explain to an Englishman, because our system of health care is so entirely different. Well, really, you *have* a system, while ours is all patch-work.'' I settled down to a lengthy explanation.

"You see, until Americans reach the age of sixty-five, they either have health insurance through their employers, who pay most of the cost with the employees contributing a little, or they pay for the insurance themselves at absolutely exorbitant rates, or they have no health insurance at all.''

"I have wondered a good deal about that. What happens if one has no insurance and becomes ill?''

"Unless it's an emergency, one stays sick. A visit to a doctor costs somewhere around seventy dollars around here, maybe twice that for a specialist. A simple prescription can easily set you back a hundred or more. Physical therapy is at least a hundred and fifty an hour, and a single day in the hospital runs around a thousand dollars, give or take, considering tests and medications and physicians' bills. Unless, of course, you require surgery, and then the sky's the limit. Nobody can afford that for anything trivial. People suffer all kinds of ailments, Alan, here in the richest country in the world, for lack of health care. Thousands die every year. They don't go to the hospital even for life-threatening problems, because they're afraid they won't be able to pay.''

Alan tried not to look shocked, but he shook his head.

"Right. It's a sin and a national shame, and something has to be done about it. But until the day comes that the politicians work it out, and I'm not holding my breath, the states have set up plans to help the truly indigent. In Indiana it's called Medicaid. It's not good, but it's better than nothing, I guess. I don't know all the rules, but I do know that you have to have virtually no assets at all to be eligible. They let you keep your house and your car—not much else.''

"You mentioned the age of sixty-five. What does that have to do with it?''

"When you're sixty-five you become eligible for Medicare. That's the national program, and it's not too bad for something run by the government. You don't have to be indigent to be eligible; it's for everyone. But it doesn't pay for everything. Specifically, it doesn't pay for medication, which is a real problem for many of the elderly. And it doesn't pay for long-term care, such as home health care or a nursing home, both of which are wildly expensive.''

I waited for the penny to drop. It didn't take long.

"So.'' Alan tented his fingers. "Kevin was running out of money. He was also rapidly approaching a time when he'd be unable to care for himself. His doctor and his priest urged him to hire someone to care for him. He would not, for very long, have been able to sustain the cost of such care.''

"Exactly. And that's where Medicaid comes in. One of the things it *does* pay for is long-term care, and you can be on Medicare and Medicaid at the same time. But as with everything run by a bureaucracy, there are catches. One of them is the indigence requirement. Well, Kevin would soon have qualified there. *But.* The other catch is that, if you've been deliberately divesting yourself of your assets during some period of time prior to your application for the aid—I don't know how long—

the state takes a very dim view. I don't know for sure whether they just deny the application or what. I know I was told, once, that they—that anonymous 'they'—state officials, I guess—go after one's debtors to try to collect the debts. I don't know if that's true or not, but it sounds like the sort of thing the state would do.''

''So that—let's see if I can work this out. Kevin had been giving away his money. He was doing so, presumably, out of sheer generosity, not in order to live on the bounty of the state. But they would have viewed it in that light, if he had applied for Medicaid.''

''I think so. Or rather, I think they wouldn't care why he did it, only *that* he did it.''

''And you think it's possible the state might have asked his debtors to repay the debts.''

''Possible, yes. I don't know for sure. Oh, mercy!''

''What, love?''

I had been talking and thinking, paying no attention to my driving. Without my conscious volition the car had turned in accustomed directions, headed down accustomed streets, nearly turned into a driveway. I pulled up to the curb and took a long, shaky breath.

''I forgot where I was going. That—that was our house.''

It didn't look quite as I remembered it, which was probably a blessing. It had been painted a sort of Wedgwood blue; we'd always kept it white. Some of the shrubs had been replaced. There was a new flower bed along one side, filled at this season with chrysanthemums. Lace curtains, instead of damask draperies, covered front windows.

''All right, darling?''

Alan reached for my hand.

I smiled at him. ''All right. Really. I thought it would

be hard, but coming up on it unexpectedly that way, I didn't have a chance to get myself all worked up. And it's different." I explained about the paint and the landscaping. "I have nothing but happy memories of that house, Alan, but they're in the past. Nothing about the present can change those memories, and there's nothing here to make me sad, or even particularly nostalgic. My house is the one in my mind, not this odd-looking blue one sitting here. This one—it's funny, but it doesn't even seem very real to me." I put the car in gear and drove away.

After some lunch to take the taste of Parson Bob out of our mouths, I settled down at the telephone. The first call was to the Medicaid office in Indianapolis.

It took a while. "I hope I'm not an old fogey," I muttered to Alan while I pushed buttons, "but I admit some modern inventions drive me crazy, and the electronic switchboard is the worst of all. Whatever became of the idea of phones being answered by real live human—oh, hello! Sorry, I thought you were going to be another recording."

I asked my questions. When they were answered, I hung up and gazed into space for a little while.

"Find out anything?"

"I'm not sure. It seems that the whole Medicaid question is a good deal more complicated than I thought." I sighed. "I'm not sure I understood everything they said, but apparently the state doesn't go after someone's debtors after all, or not in every case. If there's a genuine loan and it's being repaid regularly, they count it as a person's assets. If the loan looks uncollectible they forget about it, but if it or a gift has been made recently they instill a waiting period before the applicant can receive assistance."

Alan frowned. "A waiting period? Of how long?"

"That's where it gets really complicated. They use some formula based on the size of the loan or gift and when it was paid out. I got lost there. I think I'd have to study the guidelines to figure it out, or maybe talk to an attorney who specializes in that sort of thing."

I sighed again.

"But darling, Kevin never reached that point. So he never had to deal with the intricacies of your system— or nonsystem, as you call it."

"No, I know, but I was reaching for a motive, you see."

"Yes, of course I see." He tented his fingers. "If Kevin's debtors, or those to whom he'd made gifts, thought that the state of Indiana was about to come after them and force them to repay, one or more of them might find it a good idea to help a very old man to his reward a trifle earlier than Providence had in mind."

"Exactly. But since the state doesn't do that—"

"But you didn't know that. You thought it entirely possible."

"Yes, but—oh. If I didn't know, Kevin's debtors might not know, either."

"Exactly."

We looked at each other. "You've said all along that those loans were important."

"I said they might be. You were the one who worked out why."

I opened the notebook that lay on the table. "Four suspects. Each of them had money from Kevin in one way or another. I'm not sure our blinding insight has helped much. The motive might hold, but it applies to them all."

Alan looked over my shoulder.

"We're not sure Ms. Carmichael received any money from Kevin," he reminded me.

"That's true. I think she did, but I don't know. Oh, and anyway, Alan, she probably knows about Medicaid. What the state does, and what it doesn't do. Not all the details, maybe—that'd take a specialist—but I'll bet she knows the general outline. So if that's the motive, I think we can eliminate her. I'm glad, too. She's certainly reserved, but I rather like her. The other three, though…"

We studied the list. Mary Alice Harrison, Hannah Schneider, Bob Bussey.

"I'm still betting on him," I said finally. "And that reminds me." I looked up another number in the phone book and, after another bout with an automated phone system, had a satisfactory little talk with a representative of the Internal Revenue Service. He was most interested in my description of Parson Bob's lifestyle in contrast to that of his congregation.

"Not only tax trouble," I told Alan gleefully when I hung up the phone. "If he's really done what we think he has with the church's money, maybe state and/or federal prosecutions for theft, as well."

Alan shook his head, but he was smiling. "You're a terror, my dear. I'm extremely glad you're on my side."

I grinned. "So even if we can't prove he murdered Kevin and Jerry, we've got him on tax evasion. Sort of reminds me of Al Capone."

"And it couldn't, as you Americans like to say, happen to a nicer guy."

I giggled. Alan's attempt at a wise-guy American accent was pretty awful.

Alan laughed, too, but then it was his turn to sigh. "So far as the murders are concerned, I must confess my policeman's soul longs for even one tiny piece of concrete evidence. Dorothy, I'd like to go back to Kevin's house."

"So would I, but we can't do it now. We've got to get ready for the opera."

I WASN'T SURE WHY we were going, to tell the truth, now that Dr. Boland was out of the running as a suspect, but it still seemed somehow important. At any rate, I hoped to confront Boland and give him a piece of my mind. So we showered and dressed, Alan keeping up an undertone of disgruntled muttering the whole time, and headed out.

We covered the drive to Bloomington in record time and got to the MAC just in time to find a parking place and make the curtain comfortably. I left Alan wandering around the lobby, found my seat, and settled down to enjoy myself.

The Rake's Progress is not one of the most beloved of operas, especially for those who don't much care for twentieth-century music. I count myself in that number, but Stravinsky was an incredibly talented musician, and I enjoy some of his ballet music immensely.

I didn't have time to read the program before the lights went down; I was too busy craning my neck, trying to spot Dr. Boland in the crowd. And then the overture began and the lights dimmed and I was caught up in the great fantasy that is opera.

You wouldn't think the story of someone's decline and fall at the hands of the devil would be funny, but this one was, at least in spots. The devil (masquerading under the name of Nick Shadow) stole the show with his sarcastic humor. I even enjoyed quite a lot of the music; the soprano arias were lovely.

It got a little long, though, and by the end of the first act I was ready to join Alan in the lobby.

I found him leaning indolently on a pillar. He grinned as I approached, reminding me just a little of Nick Shadow.

"It appears that you are in need of a little liquid refreshment."

"I always said you were observant. Unfortunately, it'll have to be a soft drink. The state of Indiana takes a dim view of alcohol at its universities."

"I've already noted the offerings at the bar. With some dismay, I might add. It had best be something with caffeine in it, I think. Cola or coffee?"

"Cola, please. They haven't discovered good coffee yet."

He somehow managed to negotiate the crush around the refreshment stand and obtain a drink for me. I sipped at it. "Well, it's weak and it's too sweet and it's not very fizzy, but it's cold."

"And a stimulant. You look as though you could do with one."

I laughed and sipped a little more. "I'm just a little stiff from sitting. The opera's pretty good, actually. But I haven't seen Dr. Boland, so the evening's turned out to be something of a waste of time."

"Oh, well, if that's your trouble, turn around."

He pointed over my shoulder. There, standing alone near one of the doors to the auditorium, stood Boland.

TWENTY-FIVE

ALAN GAVE ME a little prod. "You wanted to talk to him. There he is."

Boland was reading his program. No one stood near him. There was something about his detachment that suggested not just solitude, but hostile isolation.

"Yes, but—Alan, I'm not sure about this! Do I really want to make a scene, here at a gala and all, with everybody in their best clothes?" The remark sounded silly, but Alan knew what I meant. Party clothes, party manners. "Maybe we should just go back to Hillsburg." I looked around and realized we couldn't make very rapid progress through the crowd that thronged the lobby.

And it was too late. The doctor had seen us. He folded his program with slow deliberation, put it in his pocket, and moved toward us.

I clutched Alan's arm. I must have looked trapped, for he gave my hand a reassuring pat. "Think of it this way: He can't possibly be as bad as Parson Bob," he whispered as Dr. Boland approached.

If I had thought that Stravinsky, the kind of music the man apparently liked, would have put him in a good mood, I was mistaken. He looked bleakly at both of us, not saying a word, and then shrugged.

"So you found me, Mrs. Martin. Very clever. I've

been hearing on all sides about your detective abilities. Or maybe it was your policeman husband who tracked me down. Did you intend to denounce me in front of everybody, or what?"

"We came for the opera," lied Alan blandly. "Since our paths have crossed, however, we may as well tell you that you have upset Dr. Foley considerably."

Boland shrugged again. "He'll get over it."

"How can you be so—so casual about it!" I'd forgotten my little fit of panic about confronting him, and my temper was up. "A wonderful man like that, and he's been a friend to you, and you throw him away like—like—"

"'An old shoe' is the usual expression, isn't it? Though it's not exactly appropriate here. The man was not my lover."

He bent a little closer to me; I pulled back.

"Mrs. Martin, I've been hounded from two cities. I came to your godforsaken little burg hoping to live down my past, and now you've driven me even from there."

"*I* have! What do you mean, *I*—"

"You and your snooping. People were already beginning to ask questions, to look up my record, to wonder, on account of the death of that precious old professor of yours. I had nothing to do with his death, of course. The old idiot probably inhaled particles of something ugly in that workshop of his, and no treatment known to medical science would have saved him. But you come around asking more questions, stirring up trouble, implying the old fart was murdered. Oh, yes, I had to get out of there before I was thrown out.

"I may not be the world's best doctor, but I was plenty good enough for the kind of work I was doing in Hillsburg. They'll have a hard time finding a replacement for me. And what kind of a life do you think I have ahead of me now? What does a doctor do when he can't practice anywhere? Did you ever think of that?''

The lobby lights dimmed and brightened, dimmed and brightened. The crowd moved toward the auditorium, jostling us where we stood, an island of stillness in the midst of churning motion. I looked up to make sure Alan was still right beside me, and when I looked back, Boland was gone.

I took a deep breath. "Alan, let's go."

I wished I could let Alan drive back to Hillsburg. I wanted to think. But the steep, twisting roads were a challenge even for me, and the turns we had to make weren't easy to spot at night. He let me concentrate on the road until we hit the short stretch of interstate, and then he reached out a hand and patted my knee.

"Not feeling guilty, are you?"

I stretched and tried to relax my shoulders. "No. Boland tried his best to pass the guilt on to me, but no. What's happened to him is his own fault. I'm sorry for him, though, in a way. He'll probably end up selling shoes."

"Considering the money doctors make on this side of the pond, he may never have to work again."

"And that's a pretty terrible fate for a man his age, too," I reminded him. "Years and years of nothing to do but think about his wasted life."

We were silent for the rest of the drive.

It had been a long and trying day, and we fell into bed with little conversation. Sometime in the middle of the night I half woke and moved closer to Alan, snuggling gratefully up to his comforting warmth.

Friday morning brought another perfect day. "October's bright blue weather," someone had called it.

"Oh, Alan, I wish we could spend the day playing."
I stood on our little balcony, looking out over gold-and-
bronze trees and taking deep breaths of the crisp air.
"This is my very favorite time of year."

"Do you, my dear?"

His tone was gentle. He came up behind me and put
his hands on my shoulders. "There's nothing stopping
us, you know. We could spend the day at Clifty Falls,
or in Madison doing the Tour of Homes. We could cross
the river into Kentucky, or do anything you like."

I turned and kissed him. "You know perfectly well I
couldn't enjoy it. Not yet."

"I know." He nodded matter-of-factly. "But you
needed to remind yourself."

So after a quick breakfast we took ourselves back to
Kevin's house.

"'Once more into the breach,'" Alan commented as
we got out of the car.

"'God for Harry! England and St. George,'" I re-
sponded wryly. "And we need all the help we can get,
I must say."

Somewhere between night and morning a tiny idea
had lodged itself in my brain, and I went straight to the
workshop to check it out.

I came back in a minute or two to Alan, who was
inspecting the woodstove. "Look, Alan. Wouldn't you
say that this mask would filter out most things?"

"That's rather the idea, isn't it?" he said absently,
squatting to examine the floor.

"Yes, but I thought—well, one of the things Boland
said last night was that Kevin might have inhaled something in the workshop. And I think I read somewhere
that solder could be dangerous if you inhaled the fumes,

but I guess Kevin knew that. That's what the masks were for, I suppose.''

"A pity he didn't wear one all the time," said Alan. His voice sounded very odd.

"What? What do you mean?"

Alan pulled a clean handkerchief out of his pocket, moistened a corner of it with his tongue, and scrubbed it over the floor behind the woodstove. Then he stood up.

"Smell that. Cautiously."

I sniffed and made a face. "Yuck! That's not just varnish!"

"No. It is, unless I'm very much mistaken, paint stripper.''

"Paint—you mean Kevin was trying to refinish his floor, and accidentally inhaled the fumes? But he'd have known better than that. If he was cautious enough to wear a mask in the workshop, he'd never have—"

"No, that's not what I meant at all." His voice was exceedingly grim. "Don't forget that the back of the stove is blistered as well."

"But—oh, Alan, no! What a perfectly *awful*…"

I could see it all. I could see the door opening very early on a chilly August morning, someone coming in. I could see a hand painting the jellylike stripper all over the back of the cold woodstove, dripping a little of the noxious stuff on the floor. I could see the door closing again, very quietly. I could see Kevin, perhaps with a slight cold so that his nose wasn't working very well, perhaps merely with the dimmed senses of the very old, building a fire to take off the morning chill. I could see him, a cup of steaming coffee in his hand, sitting down near the stove in his favorite chair, relaxing as the warmth soothed his old bones, basking in the comfort, and inhaling poison with every breath. Coughing a little, perhaps, blaming it on the unusually cold weather...

And very suddenly, I could see the face of the person with that murderous hand.

I took a shaky breath. Alan took me in his arms.

"We know now, don't we?" I whispered.

"We have an idea, at least."

I swallowed and looked up at him. "And I think, now, that we'll spend part of the day in Madison after all."

WE ARGUED ABOUT IT on the way. "We should leave it to the police" was Alan's opinion.

"And what would we tell them?"

"Our hypothesis."

"But that's all it is."

"Means, motive, opportunity." He intoned the litany of police investigation.

"They could all apply to anybody. We haven't narrowed it down, except in our own minds."

Alan lifted an exasperated hand and then dropped it. "Dorothy, I'm in a delicate position. I'm a guest in this country, and a senior police officer, even if a retired one, at home. I can't afford not to cooperate with the authorities."

"But, Alan, it's the authorities who haven't cooperated with us. Darryl doesn't believe a word of what we've told him, and he won't do anything about it if we tell him what we think now. As I see it, it's up to us—to me, if you like—to force the issue. Otherwise Kevin's killer is going to keep on getting away with it, and I—I couldn't stand it if that happened!"

My husband sighed. I pulled over to the side of the road, stopped, and gave him my full attention. "Look, I see your point," I said earnestly. "I'll leave you at the hotel if you want and go ahead on my own. I don't want you to get into trouble.''

He sighed again, but the twinkle was back in his eye. ''No, my dear. If you are determined to confront someone we think may have killed twice, you're not going to do it alone. Whither thou goest, et cetera.''

''Are you sure?''

''Sure. I wish you'd change your mind, but as I've never known you to do so when you've well and truly caught the scent of your prey, I'm prepared to join you in the hunt.''

''Then tally-ho!'' I said with a lightness I didn't feel, and swung the car back onto the road.

''Did you, by any chance, have a specific plan in mind? Or do you simply intend to fling an accusation into the midst of the house tour, right there in front of the good ladies of Tri Kappa? What is Tri Kappa, by the way?''

''It's a philanthropic sorority in Indiana. Something like the Women's Institute in England, if I understand *that* properly—ladies in pearls doing good works. And no, I don't have any plan. Heavens, you're right. We've got to think this thing out.''

We proceeded to do so, and by the time we were on the treacherous road heading down into Madison, we had a plan of sorts. ''There's going to be an awful lot of playing by ear in this one,'' I said dubiously.

''And when, in your criminous career, was there not?''

Well, he had a point there.

IN MADISON the Tour of Homes was in full swing. We found the Lanier mansion with no difficulty, but parking was another matter. In the end we had to park several blocks away and walk to the mansion.

There was a long line of people waiting to enter, which gave me plenty of time to get cold feet. Metaphorically, not literally. The October sun increased in strength by the minute, and we were positively hot by the time we reached the table where tickets were being sold.

One glance told me our quarry wasn't there. Two harried-looking women were selling the tickets. We bought two, donned the blue surgical bootees that were required footgear, and proceeded to tour the lovely old home at breathtaking speed. No one, guide or tourist, was very pleased with us as we whisked in and out of the many rooms.

It's a very impressive house, Greek Revival with its own exuberant Victorian touches. But I'd seen it before, of course, many times, and Alan is on visiting terms with several noble English families in their country houses, much larger and older than this one. Still, I admit it was rude of us to glance into a room, push our way back out of the crowds, and join the next group in the next room.

"You're supposed to stay with your group, you know," said one docent reprovingly.

"Yes, sorry," Alan replied with a placating smile. "Actually, we're looking for—"

"A friend," I put in hastily. "We were supposed to meet at the front door, but we seemed to have missed connections. I'm sure we'll catch up sooner or later. Oh!"

I had caught a glimpse, out a window, of a back that looked familiar. "Alan!" I pulled him away; we made for the back stairs.

The crowds were thick. The weather was gorgeous;

the tickets were expensive. The tourists were intent on seeing their fill. Without actually shoving people aside, we could make but slow progress. We finally escaped from the house and stood in the back garden, peering about us.

"Gone." I took a deep breath. "Onward!"

We headed for the next house at the nearest approach to a trot that we could manage, given the crowds, the irregular sidewalks, and our aging limbs.

"Dorothy, why are we in such a hurry?"

"I don't know. Come *on!*"

The Shrewsbury-Windle house. The Schofield house. The Demaree house. I'd never been inside most of them. I spared a bitter thought for the wasted opportunity as we rushed in and out of parlors and four-posted bedrooms, up and down curving staircases that were miracles of engineering and graceful design. We scarcely noticed them. We barely heard the docents' recitations of architects who had designed the houses and families who had lived in them.

"I shall have nightmares," Alan muttered.

"I know. It's exactly like eating a rich meal too fast. We're both going to get mental indigestion."

"If not worse."

That was a sobering thought. We pressed on.

It was at the Jeremiah Sullivan house that we finally caught up, and it was my unfortunately expressive face that undid us.

We were at the back of the crowd moving from the dining room into the serving kitchen when we saw her. She was acting as docent, standing in, I presumed, for some tired woman who was taking a break.

She saw us, too, and opened her mouth for a greeting. Then she saw the look on my face, and her own altered.

"Hello, Hannah. We've been looking for you."

TWENTY-SIX

SHE BOLTED. The tourists, bewildered at the loss of their guide, looked around at us and then back to the doorway through which she had disappeared.

"What's through there?" Alan asked urgently.

"The cellar."

"Is there a way out?"

"I don't think so."

"Let's go!"

We pushed through the crowd, uncaring now about the usual courtesies, and ran down the steep stairs.

The Sullivan house is the oldest in Madison, built circa 1818 in Federal style, very colonial in feel. The old cooking kitchen is in the cellar. It's full of wicked-looking implements made of cast iron and heavy wood. I could only guess at their original purposes. They are not, of course, meant to be touched.

Alan picked up a sharp one, I a heavy, blunt one.

The main cellar room was well lit, both by daylight from large sunken windows and by modern electric lighting. There was no place to hide. Hannah was not there.

"But where—?"

"Through there!" I pointed to the door marked "No Admittance." Footsteps sounded on the stair. An angry docent's voice floated down, shouting commands at us.

The door wasn't locked. We slipped through into the storage cellar.

I'd been in there once before with a friend who worked for Historic Madison. I hadn't liked it then. I liked it even less now.

It wasn't dark and gloomy, for it, too, had large windows. But it also had spiders. Many busy spiders. Dusty cobwebs hung everywhere, brushing one's face. I clawed one aside with a deep shudder.

There was no one in the room but ourselves.

I pointed to the little wooden door at the far end. Alan raised his eyebrows again in silent question; I shrugged. I assumed it was some kind of closet, perhaps intended originally as food storage. It was certainly the only place in the room to hide.

A cobweb dangled loosely from the top corner of the structure. That door had been opened, and recently. I was glad enough to let Alan move ahead of me and open it now.

It was empty.

"But—"

It was Alan's sharp policeman's eye that spotted the other door, the heavy door in the outside wall. It looked as though it hadn't been opened in a century or so.

Except that it, too, had a torn cobweb in one corner.

We wasted precious minutes opening the door and going up a step or two of the steep cellar stairs. It was no use. The sloping outside door was immovable.

"She's locked it!"

"Or put something heavy on top. We'll have to go the other way."

We were met in the main cellar room by outraged docents. We brushed them off, dropped our antique weapons, and sprinted up the stairs and out the back door. I would not have thought my aging knees could move that fast.

There was no clue, of course, as to which way she had gone. No helpful tourist was pointing "that-a-way." I thought fast.

"She'll have parked by the Lanier mansion. My bet is that she'll head for her car."

"I hope," said Alan, panting a little as we jogged that way, "that we can catch her up first. She's in a fragile emotional state, and one never knows…"

I put forth a little more effort and picked up the pace.

We saw her when we were a half-block away. She reached her car, tugged at the door.

The door was locked.

"Her keys must be in her purse," I said between gasps, "and she'll have tucked that away somewhere."

She looked up at the mansion, surrounded by its crowds of tourists, and at the same time saw us, nearly upon her.

She ran. Straight for the river.

I will never know how I managed that burst of speed. I can't run that fast, but I did, with Alan right beside me. We pelted down the gentle slope of gardens, raced across the street, and reached the rickety pier just as Hannah arrived at its end.

We all stopped. I think I called out to Hannah, but time at that point went into slow motion. Slowly, slowly I walked down the pier, my hand outstretched.

Slowly, slowly Hannah turned to face us, then turned away, and with the grace of a Japanese ritual, stepped out onto the air.

The splash broke the spell. I screamed. I ran to the end of the pier, Alan shouting "NO!"—and jumped into the river.

I WAS DEAD, but I was in a place of some discomfort: noisy, bright. Something tight was around my arm, something sharp pricked it. Shackles? Pitchforks? Was that Nick Shadow? Was I in…?

I drifted away.

"Dorothy."

The voice was soft and gentle. Someone was holding my hand. Reluctantly I opened my eyes again and focused on a face.

Alan's face.

"Oh. You're dead, too. How lovely."

Murmurs. An interval.

"Dorothy."

This time I saw more. The ceiling. The curtain around the bed. The IV line attached to my arm.

"What…where…?"

"You're fine, love." Alan cleared his throat. "You're doing splendidly. You're in hospital. Don't worry. Rest."

"Oh. I'm alive?"

"Yes." His voice cracked. He cleared his throat again.

"Don't go away."

"No."

They must have given me some fairly powerful sedative, because when I woke to full consciousness, the sun was streaming brightly in the window. I was sure it had been dark only a moment or two before.

"Alan!"

He had been asleep in the big recliner. He was at my side in an instant, hair wildly askew, clothes rumpled.

"Alan, tell me—"

He was kissing me before I could get out another word. It was very satisfactory.

"How are you feeling?"

I considered. "Not too bad. A little woozy, still. What did they give me, anyhow? And what happened?"

"You don't remember?"

"I remember—oh! Hannah! We were trying to stop Hannah from…" I grasped Alan's hand hard. "Alan, where's Hannah?"

"What's the last thing you can remember?"

"She was…she was running…. Was she running through the Lanier garden?"

Alan gripped my hand and looked at me with his heart in his eyes. "She was running for the river. Dorothy, love, she jumped in. You jumped in after her."

"Did I—did she—"

"You tried to save her, but you were both caught by the undertow. I managed to pull you out."

"And—?"

He shook his head.

"Maybe it was for the best," I said finally, with a gusty sigh. "I hated the idea…."

"Perhaps, yes."

"I wish, though, we'd been able to talk to her and be sure. We never had the chance to try our plan—offer her a headache pill we said we'd found in Jerry's trailer and see if she recoiled."

"You know we never thought it an especially good plan, my dear. She wasn't a dunce. If she'd planted only one capsule laced with cyanide, she'd have known the rest were perfectly harmless."

"It was all I could think of at the time. But you're right, it was pretty silly. Why on earth would we have taken anything from that filthy place? I still wish we could have tried it. I—I worry…"

"Don't, love. We're sure."

I sighed again. "I suppose we are. Her flight—"

"Not only that. I've not been idle while you've been taking your ease."

"How long have I been here?"

"The best part of twenty-four hours. Once you were snoring away—"

"I was not!"

"You were, though. And you sounded perfectly normal, and I was certain you were going to be all right, so I went to visit Darryl."

I scrunched myself up in bed. "What did he say? Was he furious?"

Alan raised the head of the bed and adjusted my pillows. "He was, but with himself, principally. He's an intelligent fellow at bottom. After he'd finished calling himself names, he launched an immediate search of Kevin's house and Jerry's trailer. Of course, Hannah's... death...made my story far more convincing."

"Hannah's suicide, Alan. We might as well be honest with ourselves."

"Not if you're working up guilt about it," he retorted. "You're quite good at that, you know, and I won't have it. Hannah was an unstable woman with a monomania. Something would have driven her over the edge eventually."

He sat on my bed looking into the distance, his fingers tented. "She was fond of Kevin, I think, in a distant sort of way, but she got it into her head that she was going to have to repay the money he'd contributed to her cause. It was substantial, by the way. We found the records. And it wasn't just the contributions. He'd also made some of his famous loans to Hannah, personally. She'd been working fewer and fewer hours, devoting all her time to the cause, and she was in fairly serious need of money."

"Just as we guessed. But you said there was proof?"

"Oh, yes, once I persuaded Darryl to look for it, his men found ample evidence of Hannah's visits to both Jerry's trailer and Kevin's house. Fibers from her clothing and a couple of her hairs behind the stove, and believe it or not, her fingerprints on the lid of the pill bottle from Jerry's kitchen counter."

"Alan! You'd have thought she'd be more careful."

"Hannah is our age, darling. Have you ever tried to manipulate the lid of a prescription bottle with gloves on? And you'll scarcely credit it, but they found Kevin's tricycle in her cellar. Tidily disassembled. I've no idea what she planned to do with it. We also found a reel of solder that looked slightly odd. We think Hannah doctored it with something to make it even more dangerous and planned to leave it in Kevin's workshop. His caution with the masks made that plan unworkable."

I shook my head sadly. "That's why she didn't want us to know she'd been in the workshop, then. Alan, it was all so unnecessary. That's what eats at me. She killed Kevin because she thought the state would take her money away, and they wouldn't have. She killed Jerry because she thought he'd seen her the morning she—did what she did—and he hadn't, or at least he never told anybody. And then she thought she had to kill herself. Three people dead, and for what?"

"They died because of Hannah's principles. Her preservation cause was more important than anything else, including human life. If someone else had got in her way, in some other fashion, he might have died, too."

I took his hand again. "You and Lord Peter said it. Principles are dangerous."

IT WAS DRIZZLING WHEN our train pulled into the Shere-bury station. We hadn't told anyone when we were coming back, so we found a taxi home. The driver's accent sounded strange. Our luggage filled up half the backseat, so I had to sit in front. I tried to get in on the right-hand side.

The garden looked bedraggled when we got to the house. Once inside, the first thing I did was turn up our new central heating.

The cats snubbed us. We had abandoned them for an eternity, and we were going to be punished. I set out some food for them; they tried to cover it up.

There was no food in the house for humans. I yawned desperately. "Alan, I'm too jet-lagged to shop, but I'm starved. We'll have to find lunch somewhere. One more restaurant meal."

"Ah, home, sweet home."

When I'm very tired, I get depressed. I plunked down on a kitchen chair and sniffled. "Home! I don't know where home is anymore. I don't seem to belong anywhere."

Alan pulled me up into a bear hug. "So far as I am concerned, my darling, you belong anywhere I am. Blow your nose and wash your face, and then we'll go find a ploughman's lunch and some real beer!"

* * * * *

Coming soon in hardcover
from WALKER AND COMPANY
And in paperback from WORLDWIDE
MYSTERY in 2002
To Perish in Penzance
by
Jeanne M. Dams